Newford Stories: Crow Girls

Charles de Lint

TRISKELL PRESS

Triskell Press
P.O. Box 9480
Ottawa, ON
Canada K1G 3V2
www.triskellpress.com

ISBN: 092062362X
ISBN-13: 978-0920623626

Cover art by Tara Larsen Chang
www.taralarsenchang.com
Cover design by MaryAnn Harris

for MaryAnn

CONTENTS

INTRODUCTION

I first came across the work of Charles de Lint in the early nineties. I'd just given birth, both to my daughter and to my second book, *Sleep, Pale Sister*, a dark little tale about ghosts and the Victorian art community. I was already writing another book, whilst working full-time as a teacher, having taken only two weeks' maternity leave. It wasn't a wonderful time for me. I had terrible headaches. I barely slept. I felt I was living a different life to the one I was meant to live; I used to look at the evening sky and dream of simply flying away.

One day I pulled out a book at random from a shelf in the city library. It was called *Memory and Dream*. As I leafed through the pages, two glossy black feathers fell out. That was my first introduction to Charles' curiously evocative, uniquely quirky, urban and yet wistful depiction of otherworldly spirits in human form, living in plain sight in those places where dream and reality intersect. I read the book, and found that it put into words thoughts I'd had about my life, but hadn't known how to articulate. It was a breath of unpolluted air; a whisper of everyday magic.

Since then I have sought out Charles' books wherever I could find them—although they are not always easy to find in the UK—and have read them with admiration and joy. No other writer does what he does in depicting the process of making art—be that painting, sculpture, writing or music. He writes with a passion and authority that only experience can give, and his words have hidden cadences that echo the rhythms of the music he loves, and conjure the secret landscapes between the world of what we know and the worlds we dare to dream.

His books are filled with characters we feel we must have met before; and maybe we have (those two feathers were certainly put there by *someone*); but in any case, the crow girls and their kind, once seen, are impossible to forget. Wild, but curiously childlike; wise and yet playful; existing outside the confines of conventional morality, and yet bringing hope and clarity to everyone whose lives they touch. Like Odin's ravens, Hugin and Munin, they seem to be an expression of our collective mind and spirit, of freedoms lost and instincts suppressed; of a simplicity of purpose and connection with the natural world that modern living has taken from us, and that we now find only in dreams, in art, in the wilderness and just occasionally, in stories like these.

This collection of Newford stories offers a glimpse behind the scenes of the everyday world into a modern dreamtime, in which the spirits of the First People cast their shadows across our lives, leaving in their wake a sense of something lost and something found—a breath of other places; a possibility of reconciliation between Man and the natural world.

Coleridge imagined a scene in which a sleeper, dreaming of Heaven, picked a flower there, only to find it in his hand as he awoke. These stories—ephemeral, bittersweet—are a reminder that what has been lost may also be re-imagined; a token of the bond between mind and spirit; body and soul; a flower picked in Paradise—

Or, just maybe, a feather.

—Joanne Harris

CROW GIRLS

I remember what somebody said about nostalgia.
He said, "It's okay to look back, as long as you
don't stare."

—Tom Paxton,
from an interview with Ken Rockburn

People have a funny way of remembering where they've been, who they were. Facts fall by the wayside. Depending on their temperament, they either remember a golden time when all was better than well, better than it can be again, better than it ever really was: a first love, the endless expanse of a summer vacation, youthful vigor, the sheer novelty of being alive that gets lost when the world starts wearing you down. Or they focus in on the bad, blow little incidents all out of proportion, hold grudges for years, or maybe they really did have some unlucky times, but now they're reliving them forever in their heads instead of moving on.

But the brain plays tricks on us all, doesn't it? We go by what it tells us, have to, I suppose, because what else do we have to use as touchstones? Trouble is, we don't ask for confirmation on what the brain tells us. Things don't have to be real, we just have to believe they're real, which pretty much explains politics and religion as much as it does what goes on inside our heads.

Don't get me wrong; I'm not pointing any fingers here. My people aren't guiltless either. The only difference is our memories go back a lot further than yours do.

* * *

"I don't get computers," Heather said.

Jilly laughed. "What's not to get?"

They were having cappuccinos in the Cyberbean Café, sitting at the long counter with computer terminals spaced along its length the way those little individual jukeboxes used to be in highway diners. Jilly looked as though she'd been using the tips of her dark ringlets as paintbrushes, then cleaned them on the thighs of her jeans—in other words, she'd come straight from the studio without changing first. But however haphazardly messy she might allow herself or her studio to get, Heather knew she'd either cleaned her brushes, or left them soaking in turps before coming down to the café. Jilly might seem terminally easygoing, but some things she didn't blow off. No matter how the work was going—good, bad or indifferent—she treated her tools with respect.

As usual, Jilly's casual scruffiness made Heather feel

6

overdressed. She was only wearing cotton pants and a blouse, nothing fancy. But she always felt a little like that around Jilly, ever since she'd first taken a class from her at the Newford School of Art a couple of winters ago. No matter how hard she tried, she hadn't been able to shake the feeling that she looked so typical: the suburban working mother, the happy wife. The differences since she and Jilly had first met weren't great. Her blond hair had been long then, while now it was cropped short. She was wearing glasses now instead of her contacts.

And two years ago she hadn't been carrying an empty wasteland around inside her chest.

"Besides," Jilly added. "You use a computer at work, don't you?"

"Sure, but that's work," Heather said. "Not games and computer screen romances and stumbling around the Internet, looking for information you're never going to find a use for outside of Trivial Pursuit."

"I think it's bringing back a sense of community," Jilly said.

"Oh, right."

"No, think about it. All these people who might have been just vegging out in front of a TV are chatting with each other in cyberspace instead—hanging out, so to speak, with kindred spirits that they might never have otherwise met."

Heather sighed. "But it's not real human contact."

"No. But at least it's contact."

"I suppose."

Jilly regarded her over the brim of her glass coffee mug. It was a mild gaze, not in the least probing, but Heather couldn't help but feel as though Jilly were seeing right inside her head, all the way down to where desert winds blew through the empty space where her heart had been.

"So what's the real issue?" Jilly asked.

Heather shrugged. "There's no issue." She took a sip of her own coffee, then tried on a smile. "I'm thinking of moving downtown."

"Really?"

"Well, you know. I already work here. There's a good school for the kids. It just seems to make sense."

"How does Peter feel about it?"

Heather hesitated for a long moment, then sighed again. "Peter's not really got anything to say about it."

"Oh, no. You guys always seemed so..." Jilly's voice trailed off. "Well, I guess you weren't really happy, were you?"

"I don't know what we were anymore. I just know we're not together. There wasn't a big blowup or anything. He wasn't cheating on me and I certainly wasn't cheating on him. We're just...not together."

"It must be so weird."

Heather nodded. "Very weird. It's a real shock, suddenly discovering after all these years that we really don't have much in common at all."

Jilly's eyes were warm with sympathy. "How are you holding up?"

"Okay, I suppose. But it's so confusing. I don't know what to think, who I am, what I thought I was doing with the last twenty years of my life. I mean, I don't regret the girls—I'd have had more children if we could have had them—but everything else…"

She didn't know how to begin to explain.

"I married Peter when I was eighteen and I'm forty-one now. I've been a part of a couple for longer than I've been anything else, but except for the girls, I don't know what any of it meant anymore. I don't know who I am. I thought we'd be together forever, that we'd grow old together, you know? But now it's just me. Casey's fifteen and Janice is twelve. I've got another few years of being a mother, but after that, who am I? What am I going to do with myself?"

"You're still young," Jilly said. "And you look gorgeous."

"Right."

"Okay. A little pale today, but still."

Heather shook her head. "I don't know why I'm telling you this. I haven't told anybody."

"Not even your mom or your sister?"

"Nobody. It's…"

She could feel tears welling up, the vision blurring, but she made herself take a deep breath. It seemed to help. Not a lot, but some. Enough to carry on. How to explain why she wanted to keep it a secret? It wasn't as though it was something she could keep hidden forever.

"I think I feel like a failure," she said.

Her voice was so soft she almost couldn't hear herself, but Jilly reached over and took her hand.

"You're not a failure. Things didn't work out, but that doesn't mean it was your fault. It takes two people to make or break a relationship."

"I suppose. But to have put in all those years…"

Jilly smiled. "If nothing else, you've got two beautiful daughters to show for them."

Heather nodded. The girls certainly did a lot to keep the emptiness at bay, but once they were in bed asleep and she was by herself, alone in the dark, sitting on the couch by the picture window, staring down the street at all those other houses just like her own, that desolate place inside her seemed to go on forever.

She took another sip of her coffee and looked past Jilly to where two young women were sitting at a corner table, heads bent together, whispering. It was hard to place their ages— anywhere from late teens to early twenties, sisters, perhaps, with their small builds and similar dark looks, their black clothing and short blue-black hair. For no reason she could explain, simply seeing them made her feel a little better.

"Remember what it was like to be so young?" she said.

Jilly turned, following her gaze, then looked back at Heather.

"You never think about stuff like this at that age," Heather went on.

"I don't know," Jilly said. "Maybe not. But you have a thousand other anxieties that probably feel way more catastrophic."

"You think?"

Jilly nodded. "I know. We all like to remember it as a perfect time, but most of us were such bundles of messed-up hormones and nerves I'm surprised we ever managed to reach twenty."

"I suppose. But still, looking at those girls…"

Jilly turned again, leaning her head on her arm. "I know what you mean. They're like a piece of summer on a cold winter's morning."

It was a perfect analogy, Heather thought, especially considering the winter they'd been having. Not even the middle of December and the snowbanks were already higher than her chest, the temperature a seriously cold minus fifteen.

"I have to remember their faces," Jilly went on. "For when I get back to the studio. The way they're leaning so close to each other—like confidantes, sisters in their hearts, if not by blood. And look at the fine bones in their features...how dark their eyes are."

Heather nodded. "It'd make a great picture."

It would, but the thought of it depressed her. She found herself yearning desperately in that one moment to have had an entirely different life, it almost didn't matter what. Perhaps one that had no responsibility but to draw great art from the world around her, the way Jilly did. If she hadn't had to support Peter while he was going through law school, maybe she would have stuck with her art....

Jilly swiveled in her chair, the sparkle in her eyes deepening into concern once more.

"Anything you need, anytime," she said. "Don't be afraid to call me."

Heather tried another smile. "We could chat on the Internet."

"I think I agree with what you said earlier: I like this better."

"Me too," Heather said. Looking out the window, she added,

11

"It's snowing again."

* * *

Maida and Zia are forever friends. Crow girls with spiky blue-black hair and eyes so dark it's easy to lose your way in them. A little raggedy and never quiet, you can't miss this pair: small and wild and easy in their skins, living on Zen time. Sometimes they forget they're crows, left their feathers behind in the long ago, and sometimes they forget they're girls. But they never forget that they're friends.

People stop and stare at them wherever they go, borrowing a taste of them, drawn by they don't know what, they just have to look, try to get close, but keeping their distance, too, because there's something scary/craving about seeing animal spirits so pure walking around on a city street. It's a shock, like plunging into cold water at dawn, waking up from the comfortable familiarity of warm dreams to find, if only for a moment, that everything's changed. And then, just before the way you know the world to be comes rolling back in on you, maybe you hear giddy laughter, or the slow flap of crows' wings. Maybe you see a couple of dark-haired girls sitting together in the corner of a café, heads bent together, pretending you can't see them, or could be they're perched on a tree branch, looking down at you looking up, working hard at putting on serious faces but they can't stop smiling.

It's like that rhyme, "two for mirth." They can't stop smiling and neither can you. But you've got to watch out for crow girls. Sometimes they wake a yearning you'll be hard-pressed to put back to sleep. Sometimes only a glimpse of them can start up a familiar ache deep in your chest, an ache you can't name, but you've felt it before, early mornings, lying alone in your bed, trying to hold on to the fading tatters of a perfect dream. Sometimes they blow bright the coals of a longing that can't ever be eased.

* * *

Heather couldn't stop thinking of the two girls she'd seen in the café earlier in the evening. It was as though they'd lodged pieces of themselves inside her, feathery slivers winging dreamily across the wasteland. Long after she'd played a board game with Janice, then watched the end of a Barbara Walters special with Casey, she found herself sitting up by the big picture window in the living room when she should be in bed herself. She regarded the street through a veil of falling snow, but this time she wasn't looking at the houses, so alike except for the varying heights of their snowbanks, they might as well all be the same one. Instead, she was looking for two small women with spiky black hair, dark shapes against the white snow.

There was no question but that they knew exactly who they were, she thought when she realized what she was doing. Maybe they could tell her who she was. Maybe they could come up with an exotic past for her so that she could reinvent herself, be someone like them, free, sure of herself. Maybe they could at least tell her where she was going.

But there were no thin, dark-haired girls out on the snowy street, and why should there be? It was too cold. Snow was falling thick with another severe winter storm warning in effect tonight. Those girls were safe at home. She knew that. But she kept looking for them all the same because in her chest she could feel the beat of dark wings—not the sudden panic that came out of nowhere when once again the truth of her situation reared without warning in her mind, but a strange, alien feeling. A sense that some otherness was calling to her.

The voice of that otherness scared her almost more than the grey landscape lodged in her chest.

She felt she needed a safety net to be able to let herself go and not have to worry about where she fell. Someplace where she didn't have to think, be responsible, to do anything. Not forever. Just for a time.

She knew Jilly was right about nostalgia. The memories she carried forward weren't necessarily the way things had really happened. But she yearned, if only for a moment, to be able to relive some of those simpler times, those years in high school before she'd met Peter, before they were married, before her emotions got so complicated.

And then what?

You couldn't live in the past. At some point you had to come up for air and then the present would be waiting for you, unchanged. The wasteland in her chest would still stretch on forever. She'd still be trying to understand what had happened. Had Peter changed? Had she changed? Had they both changed? And when did it happen? How much of their life together had been a lie?

It was enough to drive her mad.

It was enough to make her want to step into the otherness calling to her from out there in the storm and snow, step out and simply let it swallow her whole.

* * *

Jilly couldn't put the girls from the café out of her mind either, but for a different reason. As soon as she'd gotten back to the studio, she'd taken her current work-in-progress down from the easel and replaced it with a fresh canvas. For a long moment she stared at the texture of the pale ground, a mix of gesso and a light burnt ochre acrylic wash, then she took up a stick of charcoal and began to sketch the faces of the two dark-haired girls before the memory of them left her mind.

She was working on their bodies, trying to capture the loose splay of their limbs and the curve of their backs as they'd slouched in toward each other over the café table, when there came a knock at her door.

"It's open," she called over her shoulder, too intent on what she was doing to look away.

"I could've been some mad, psychotic killer," Geordie said as he came in.

He stamped his feet on the mat, brushed the snow from his shoulders and hat. Setting his fiddle case down by the door, he went over to the kitchen counter to see if Jilly had any coffee on.

"But instead," Jilly said, "it's only a mad, psychotic fiddler, so I'm entirely safe."

"There's no coffee."

"Sure there is. It's just waiting for you to make it."

Geordie put on the kettle, then rummaged around in the fridge, trying to find which tin Jilly was keeping her coffee beans in this week. He found them in one that claimed to hold Scottish shortbreads.

"You want some?" he asked.

Jilly shook her head. "How's Tanya?"

"Heading back to L.A. I just saw her off at the airport. The driving's horrendous. There were cars in the ditch every couple hundred feet and I thought the bus would never make it back."

"And yet, it did," Jilly said.

Geordie smiled.

"And then," she went on, "because you were feeling bored and lonely, you decided to come visit me at two o'clock in the morning."

"Actually, I was out of coffee and I saw your light was on." He crossed the loft and came around behind the easel so that he could see what she was working on. "Hey, you're doing the crow girls."

"You know them?"

Geordie nodded. "Maida and Zia. You've caught a good likeness of them—especially Zia. I love that crinkly smile of hers."

"You can tell them apart?"

"You can't?"

"I never saw them before tonight. Heather and I were in the Cyberbean and there they were, just asking to be drawn." She added a bit of shading to the underside of a jaw, then turned to look at Geordie. "Why do you call them the crow girls?"

Geordie shrugged. "I don't. Or at least I didn't until I was talking to Jack Daw and that's what he called them when they came sauntering by. The next time I saw them I was busking in front of St. Paul's, so I started to play 'The Blackbird,' just to

16

see what would happen, and sure enough, they came over to talk to me."

"Crow girls," Jilly repeated. The name certainly fit.

"They're some kind of relation to Jack," Geordie explained, "but I didn't quite get it. Cousins, maybe."

Jilly was suddenly struck with the memory of a long conversation she'd had with Jack one afternoon. She was working up sketches of the Crowsea Public Library for a commission when he came and sat beside her on the grass. With his long legs folded under him, black brimmed hat set at a jaunty angle, he'd regaled her with a long, rambling discourse on what he called the continent's real First Nations.

"Animal people," she said softly.

Geordie smiled. "I see he fed you that line, too."

But Jilly wasn't really listening—not to Geordie. She was remembering another part of that old conversation, something else Jack had told her.

"The thing we really don't get," he'd said, leaning back in the grass, "is these contracted families you have. The mother, the father, the children, all living alone in some big house. Our families extend as far as our bloodlines and friendship can reach."

"I don't know much about bloodlines," Jilly said. "But I know about friends."

He'd nodded. "That's why I'm talking to you."

Jilly blinked and looked at Geordie. "It made sense what he said."

Geordie smiled. "Of course it did. Immortal animal people."

"That, too. But I was talking about the weird way we think about families and children. Most people don't even like kids—don't want to see, hear, or hear about them. But when you look at other cultures, even close to home...up on the rez, in Chinatown, Little Italy...it's these big rambling extended families, everybody taking care of everybody else."

Geordie cleared his throat. Jilly waited for him to speak but he went instead to unplug the kettle and finish making the coffee. He ground up some beans and the noise of the hand-cranked machine seemed to reach out and fill every corner of the loft. When he stopped, the sudden silence was profound, as though the city outside were holding its breath along with the inheld breath of the room. Jilly was still watching him when he looked over at her.

"We don't come from that kind of family," he said finally.

"I know. That's why we had to make our own."

* * *

It's late at night, snow whirling in dervishing gusts, and the crow girls are perched on top of the wooden fence that's been erected around a work site on Williamson Street. Used to be a parking lot there, now it's a big hole in the ground on its way to being one more office complex that nobody except the contractors wants. The top of the fence is barely an inch wide and slippery with snow, but they have no trouble balancing there.

Zia has a ring with a small spinning disc on it. Painted on the disc is a psychedelic coil that goes spiraling down into infinity. She keeps spinning it and the two of them stare down into the faraway place at the center of the spiral until the disc slows down, almost stops. Then Zia gives it another flick with her fingernail, and the coil goes spiraling down again.

"Where'd you get this anyway?" Maida asks.

Zia shrugs. "Can't remember. Found it somewhere."

"In someone's pocket."

"And you never did?"

Maida grins. "Just wish I'd seen it first, that's all."

They watch the disc some more, content.

"What do you think it's like down there?" Zia says after a while. "On the other side of the spiral."

Maida has to think about that for a moment. "Same as here," she finally announces, then winks. "Only dizzier."

They giggle, leaning into each other, tottering back and forth on their perch. Crow girls can't be touched, can't hardly be seen, except someone's standing down there on the sidewalk, looking up through the falling snow, his worried expression so comical it sets them off on a new round of giggles.

"Careful now!" he calls up to them. He thinks they're on drugs—they can tell. "You don't want to—"

Before he can finish, they hold hands and let themselves fall backward , off the fence.

"Oh, Christ!"

He jumps, gets a handhold on the top of the fence and hauls himself up. But when he looks over, over and down, way down, there's nothing to be seen. No girls lying at the bottom of that big hole in the ground, nothing at all. Only the falling snow. It's like they were never there.

His arms start to ache and he lowers himself back down

19

the fence, lets go, bending his knees slightly to absorb the impact of the last couple of feet. He slips, catches his balance. It seems very still for a moment, so still he can hear an odd rhythmical whispering sound. Like wings. He looks up, but there's too much snow coming down to see anything. A cab comes by, skidding on the slick street, and he blinks. The street's full of city sounds again, muffled, but present. He hears the murmuring conversation of a couple approaching him, their shoulders and hair white with snow. A snowplow a few streets over. A distant siren.

He continues along his way, but he's walking slowly now, trudging through the drifts, not thinking so much of two girls sitting on top of a fence as remembering how, when he was a boy, he used to dream that he could fly.

* * *

After fiddling a little more with her sketch, Jilly finally put her charcoal down. She made herself a cup of herbal tea with the leftover hot water in the kettle and joined Geordie where he was sitting on the sofa, watching the snow come down. It was warm in the loft, almost cozy compared to the storm on the other side of the windowpanes, or maybe because of the storm. Jilly leaned back on the sofa, enjoying the companionable silence for a while before she finally spoke.

"How do you feel after seeing the crow girls?" she asked.

Geordie turned to look at her. "What do you mean, how do I feel?"

"You know, good, bad…different…"

Geordie smiled. "Don't you mean 'indifferent'?"

"Maybe." She picked up her tea from the crate where

20

she'd set it and took a sip. "Well?" she asked when he didn't continue.

"Okay. How do I feel? Good, I suppose. They're fun, they make me smile. In fact, just thinking of them now makes me feel good."

Jilly nodded thoughtfully as he spoke. "Me too. And something else as well."

"The different," Geordie began. He didn't quite sigh. "You believe those stories of Jack's, don't you?"

"Of course. And you don't?"

"I'm not sure," he replied, surprising her.

"Well, I think these crow girls were in the Cyberbean for a purpose," Jilly said. "Like in that rhyme about crows."

Geordie got it right away. "Two for mirth."

Jilly nodded. "Heather needed some serious cheering up. Maybe even something more. You know how when you start feeling low, you can get on this descending spiral of depression…everything goes wrong, things get worse because you expect them to?"

"Fight it with the power of positive thinking, I always say."

"Easier said than done when you're feeling that low. What you really need at a time like that is something completely unexpected to kick you out of it and remind you that there's more to life than the hopeless, grey expanse you think is stretching in every direction. What Colin Wilson calls 'absurd good news.'"

"You've been talking to my brother."

"It doesn't matter where I got it from—it's still true."

Geordie shook his head. "I don't buy the idea that Maida and Zia showed up just to put your friend in a better mood. Even bird people can get a craving for a cup of coffee, can't they?"

"Well, yes," Jilly said. "But that doesn't preclude their being there for Heather, as well. Sometimes when a person needs something badly enough, it just comes to them. A personal kind of steam engine time. You might not be able to articulate what it is you need, you might not even know you need something—at least, not at a conscious level—but the need's still there, calling out to whatever's willing to listen."

Geordie smiled. "Like animal spirits."

"Crow girls."

Geordie shook his head. "Drink your tea and go to bed," he told her. "I think you need a good night's sleep."

"But—"

"It was only a coincidence. Things don't always have a meaning. Sometimes they just happen. And besides, how do you even know they had any effect on Heather?"

"I could just tell. And don't change the subject."

"I'm not."

"Okay," Jilly said. "But don't you see? It doesn't matter if it was a coincidence or not. They still showed up when Heather needed them. It's more of that 'small world, spooky world' stuff Professor Dapple goes on about. Everything's connected. It doesn't matter if we can't see how, it's still all connected. You know, chaos theory and all that."

Geordie shook his head, but he was smiling. "Does it ever strike you as weird when something Bramley's talked up for years suddenly becomes an acceptable element of scientific study?"

"Nothing strikes me as truly weird," Jilly told him. "There's only stuff I haven't figured out yet."

* * *

Heather barely slept that night. For the longest time she simply couldn't sleep, and then when she finally did, she was awake by dawn. Wide awake, but heavy with an exhaustion that came more from heartache than lack of sleep.

Sitting up against the headboard, she tried to resist the sudden tightness in her chest, but that sad, cold wasteland swelled inside her. The bed seemed depressingly huge. She didn't so much miss Peter's presence as feel adrift in the bed's expanse of blankets and sheets. Adrift in her life. Why was it he seemed to have no trouble carrying on, when the simple act of getting up in the morning felt as though it would require far more energy than she could ever hope to muster?

She stared at the snow swirling against her window, not at all relishing the drive into town on a morning like this. If anything, it was coming down harder than it had been last night. All it took was the suggestion of snow and everybody in the city seemed to forget how to drive, never mind common courtesy or traffic laws. A blizzard like this would snarl traffic and back it up as far as the mountains.

She sighed, supposing it was just as well she'd woken so early since it would take her at least an extra hour to get downtown today.

Up, she told herself, and forced herself to swing her feet to the floor and rise. A shower helped. It didn't really ease the heartache, but the hiss of the water made it easier to ignore her thoughts. Coffee, when she was dressed and had brewed a pot, helped more, though she still winced when Janice came bounding into the kitchen.

"It's a snow day!" she cried. "No school. They just announced it on the radio. The school's closed, closed, closed!"

She danced about in her flannel nightie, pirouetting in the small space between the counter and the table.

"Just yours," Heather asked, "or Casey's, too?"

"Mine, too," Casey replied, following her sister into the room.

Unlike Janice, she was maintaining her cool, but Heather could tell she was just as excited. Too old to allow herself to take part in Janice's spontaneous celebration, but young enough to be feeling giddy with the unexpected holiday.

"Good," Heather said. "You can look after your sister."

"*Mom!*" Janice protested. "I'm not a baby."

"I know. It's just good to have someone older in the house when—"

"You can't be thinking of going in to work today," Casey said.

"We could do all kinds of stuff," Janice added. "Finish decorating the house. Baking."

"Yeah," Casey said, "all the things we don't seem to have time for anymore."

Heather sighed. "The trouble is," she explained, "the real world doesn't work like school. We don't get snow days."

Casey shook her head. "That is *so* unfair."

The phone rang before Heather could agree.

"I'll bet it's your boss," Janice said as Heather picked up the phone. "Calling to tell you it's a snow day for you, too."

Don't I wish, Heather thought. But then what would she do at home all day? It was so hard being here, even with the girls and as much as she loved them. Everywhere she turned, something reminded her of how the promises of a good life had turned into so much ash. At least work kept her from brooding. She brought the receiver up to her ear and spoke into the mouthpiece.

"Hello?"

"I've been thinking," the voice on the other end of the line said. "About last night."

Heather had to smile. Wasn't that so Jilly, calling up first thing in the morning as though they were still in the middle of last night's conversation.

"What about last night?" she said.

"Well, all sorts of stuff. Like remembering a perfect moment in the past and letting it carry you through a hard time now."

If only, Heather thought. "I don't have a moment that perfect," she said.

"I sort of got that feeling," Jilly told her. "That's why I think they were a message—a kind of perfect moment now, that you can use the same way."

"What *are* you talking about?"

"The crow girls. In the café last night."

"The crow…" It took her a moment to realize what Jilly meant. Their complexions had been dark enough so she supposed they could have been Indians.

"How do you know what tribe they belonged to?"

"Not crow, Native American," Jilly said, "but crow, bird people."

Heather shook her head as she listened to what Jilly went on to say, for all that only her daughters were there to see the movement. Glum looks had replaced their earlier excitement when they realized the call wasn't from her boss.

"Do you have any idea how improbable all of this sounds?" she asked when Jilly finished. "Life's not like your paintings."

"Says who?"

"How about common sense?"

"Tell me," Jilly said. "Where did common sense ever get you?"

Heather sighed. "Things don't happen just because we want them to," she said.

"Sometimes that's *exactly* why they happen," Jilly replied. "They happen because we need them to."

"I don't live in that kind of a world."

"But you could."

Heather looked across the kitchen at her daughters once more. The girls were watching her, trying to make sense out of the one-sided conversation they were hearing. Heather wished them luck. She was hearing both sides and that didn't seem to help at all. You couldn't simply reinvent your world because you wanted to. Things just were how they were.

"Just think about it," Jilly added. "Will you do that much?"

"I..."

That bleak landscape inside Heather seemed to expand, growing so large there was no way she could contain it. She focused on the faces of her daughters. She remembered the crow girls in the café. There was so much innocence in them all, daughters and crow girls. She'd been just like them once and she knew it wasn't simply nostalgia colouring her memory. She knew there'd been a time when she lived inside each particular day, on its own and by itself, instead of trying to deal with all the days of her life at once, futilely attempting to reconcile the discrepancies and mistakes.

"I'll try," she said into the phone.

They said their goodbyes and Heather slowly cradled the receiver.

"Who was that, Mom?" Casey asked.

Heather looked out the window. The snow was still falling, muffling the world. Covering its complexities with a blanket as innocent as the hope she saw in her daughters' eyes.

"Jilly," she said. She took a deep breath, then smiled at them. "She was calling to tell me that today really is a snow day."

The happiness that flowered on their faces helped ease the tightness in her chest. The grey landscape waiting for her there didn't go away, but for some reason, it felt less profound. She wasn't even worried about what her boss would say when she called to tell him she wouldn't be in today.

* * *

Crow girls can move like ghosts. They'll slip into your house when you're not home, sometimes when you're only sleeping, go walking spirit-soft through your rooms and hallways, sit in your favourite chair, help themselves to cookies and beer, borrow a trinket or two which they'll mean to return and usually do. It's not break-and-enter so much as simple curiosity. They're worse than cats.

Privacy isn't in their nature. They don't seek it and barely understand the concept. Personal property is even more alien. The idea of ownership—that one can lay proprietary claim to a piece of land, an object, another person or creature—doesn't even register.

"Whatcha looking at?" Zia asks.

They don't know whose house they're in. Walking along on the street, trying to catch snowflakes on their tongues, one or the other of them suddenly got the urge to come inside. Upstairs, the family sleeps.

Maida shows her the photo album. "Look," she says. "It's the same people, but they keep changing. See, here's she's a baby, then she's a little girl, then a teenager."

"Everything changes," Zia says. "Even we get old. Look at Crazy Crow."

"But it happens so fast with them."

Zia sits down beside her and they pore over the pictures, munching on apples they found earlier in a cold cellar in the basement.

Upstairs, a father wakes in his bed. He stares at the ceiling, wondering what woke him. Nervous energy crackles inside him like static electricity, a sudden spill of adrenaline, but he doesn't know why. He gets up and checks the children's rooms. They're both asleep. He listens for intruders, but the house is silent.

Stepping back into the hall, he walks to the head of the stairs and looks down. He thinks he sees something in the gloom, two dark-haired girls sitting on the sofa, looking through a photo album. Their gazes lift to meet his and hold it. The next thing he knows, he's on the sofa himself, holding the photo album in his hand. There are no strange girls sitting there with him. The house seems quieter than it's ever been, as though the fridge, the furnace and every clock the family owns are holding their breath along with him.

He sets the album down on the coffee table, walks slowly back up the stairs and returns to his bed. He feels like a stranger, misplaced. He doesn't know this room, doesn't know the woman beside him. All he can think about is the first girl he ever loved and his heart swells with a bittersweet sorrow. An ache pushes against his ribs, makes it almost impossible to breathe.

What if, what if…

He turns on his side and looks at his wife. For one moment her face blurs, becomes a morphing image that encompasses both her features and those of his first true love. For one moment it seems as though anything is possible, that for all these years he could have been married to another woman, to that girl who first held, then unwittingly, broke his heart.

"No," he says.

His wife stirs, her features her own again. She blinks sleepily at him.

"Wha…?" she mumbles.

He holds her close, heartbeat drumming, more in love

with her for being who she is than he has ever been before.

Outside, the crow girls are lying on their backs, making snow angels on his lawn, scissoring their arms and legs, shaping skirts and wings. They break their apple cores in two and give their angels eyes, then run off down the street, holding hands. The snowdrifts are undisturbed by their weight. It's as though they, too, like the angels they've just made, have wings.

* * *

"This is so cool," Casey tells her mother. "It really feels like Christmas. I mean, not like Christmases we've had, but, you know, like really being part of Christmas."

Heather nods. She's glad she brought the girls down to the soup kitchen to help Jilly and her friends serve a Christmas dinner to those less fortunate than themselves. She's been worried about how her daughters would take the break from tradition, but then realized, with Peter gone, tradition is already broken. Better to begin all over again.

The girls had been dubious when she first broached the subject with them—"I don't want to spend Christmas with *losers*," had been Casey's first comment. Heather hadn't argued with her. All she'd said was, "I want you to think about what you just said."

Casey's response had been a sullen look—there were more and more of these lately—but Heather knew her own daughter well enough. Casey had stomped off to her room, but then come back half an hour later and helped her explain to Janice why it might not be the worst idea in the world.

She watches them now, Casey having rejoined her sister where they are playing with the homeless children, and knows a swell of pride. They're such good kids, she thinks as she takes another sip of her cider. After a couple of hours serving coffee, tea and hot cider, she'd really needed to get off her feet for a moment.

"Got something for you," Jilly says, sitting down on the bench beside her.

Heather accepts the small, brightly-wrapped parcel with reluctance. "I thought we said we weren't doing Christmas presents."

"It's not really a Christmas present. It's more an everyday sort of a present that I just happen to be giving you today."

"Right."

"So aren't you going to open it?"

Heather peels back the paper and opens the small box. Inside, nestled in a piece of folded Kleenex, are two small silver earrings cast in the shapes of crows. Heather lifts her gaze.

"They're beautiful."

"Got them at the craft show from a local jeweler. Rory Crowther. See, his name's on the card in the bottom of the box. They're to remind you—"

Heather smiles. "Of crow girls?"

"Partly. But more to remember that this—" Jilly waves a hand that could be taking in the basement of St. Vincent's, could be taking in the whole world. "It's not all we get. There's more. We can't always see it, but it's there."

For a moment, Heather thinks she sees two dark-haired slim figures standing on the far side of the basement, but when she looks more closely they're only a bag lady and Geordie's friend Tanya, talking.

For a moment, she thinks she hears the sound of wings, but it's only the murmur of conversation. Probably.

What she knows for sure is that the grey landscape inside her chest is shrinking a little more every day.

"Thank you," she says.

She isn't sure if she's speaking to Jilly or to crow girls she's only ever seen once, but whose presence keeps echoing through her life. Her new life. It isn't necessarily a better one. Not yet. But at least it's on the way up from wherever she'd been going, not down into a darker despair.

"Here," Jilly says. "Let me help you put them on."

TWA CORBIES

As I was walkin' all alane
I heard twa corbies makin' mane...
    —from "Twa Corbies,"
    Scots traditional

Gerda couldn't sleep again. She stood by the upright piano, wedding picture in hand, marvelling at how impossibly young she and Jan had been. Why, they were little more than children. Imagine making so serious a commitment at such an age, raising a family and all.

Her insomnia had become a regular visitor over the past few years—often her only one. The older she got, the less sleep she seemed to need. She went to bed late, got up early, and the only weariness she carried through her waking hours was in her heart. A loneliness that was stronger some nights than others.

But on those nights, the old four-poster double bed felt too big for her. All that extra room spread over the map of the quilt like unknown territories, encroaching on her ability to relax, even with the cats lolling across the hills and vales of the bed's expanse.

It hadn't always been that way. When Jan was still alive—before the children were born, and after they'd moved out to accept the responsibility of their own lives—she and Jan could spend the whole day in bed, passing the time with long conversations and silly little jokes, sharing tea and biscuits while they read the paper, making slow and sweet love…

She sighed. But Jan was long gone and she was an old woman with only her cats and piano to keep her company now. This late at night, the piano could offer her no comfort—it wouldn't be fair to her neighbours. The building was like her, old and worn. The sound of the piano would carry no matter how softly she played. But the cats…

One of them was twining in and out against her legs now—Swarte Meg, the youngest of the three. She was just a year old, black as the night sky, as gangly and unruly as a pumpkin vine. Unlike the other two, she still craved regular attention and loved to be carried around in Gerda's arms. It made even the simplest of tasks difficult to attend to, but there was nothing in Gerda's life that required haste anymore.

Replacing the wedding picture on the top of the piano, she picked Swarte Meg up and moved over to the window that provided her with a view of the small, cobblestoned square outside.

By day there was always someone to watch. Mothers and

nannies with their children, sitting on the bench and chatting with each other while their charges slept in prams. Old men smoking cigarettes, pouring coffee for each other out of a thermos, playing checkers and dominoes. Neighbourhood gossips standing by the river wall, exaggerating their news to give it the desired impact. Tourists wandering into the square and looking confused, having wandered too far from the more commercial streets.

By this time of night, all that changed. Now the small square was left to fend for itself. It seemed diminished, shadows pooling deep against the buildings, held back only by the solitary street lamp that rose up behind the wrought iron bench at its base.

Except…

Gerda leaned closer to the windowpane.

What was this…?

- 2 -

Sophie's always telling me to pace myself. The trouble is, when I get absorbed in a piece, I can spend whole days in front of the canvas, barely stopping to eat or rest until the day's work is done. My best times, though, are early in the morning and late at night—morning for the light, the late hours for the silence. The phone doesn't ring, no one knocks on your door. I usually seem to finish a piece at night. I know I have to see it again in the morning light, so to stop myself from fiddling with it, I go out walking—anywhere, really.

When the work's gone well, I can feel a deep thrumming

build up inside me and I wouldn't be able to sleep if I wanted to, doesn't matter how tired I might be. What I need then is for the quiet streets of the city and the swell of the dark night above them to pull me out of myself and my painting. To render calm to my quickened pulse. Walking puts a peace in my soul that I desperately need after having had my nose up close to a canvas for far too long.

Any part of the city will do, but Old Market's the best. I love it here, especially at this time of night. There's a stillness in the air and even the houses and shops seem to be holding their breath. All I can hear is the sound of my boots on the cobblestones. One day I'm going to move into one of the old brick buildings that line these streets—it doesn't matter which one; I love them all. As much for where they are, I suppose, as for what they are.

Because Old Market's a funny place. It's right downtown, but when you step into its narrow, cobblestoned streets, it's like you've stepped back in time to an older, other place. The rhythms are different here. The sound of traffic seems to disappear far more quickly than should be physically possible. The air tastes cleaner and it still carries hints of baking bread, Indonesian spices, cabbage soups, fish and sausages long after midnight.

On a night like this I don't even bother to change. I just go out in my paint-stained clothes, the scent of my turps and linseed trailing along behind me. I don't worry about how I look because there's no one to see me. By now, all the cafés are closed up and except for the odd cat, everybody's in bed, or checking out the nightlife downtown. Or almost everybody.

I hear the sound of their wings first—loud in the stillness. Then I see them, a pair of large crows that swoop down out of the sky to dart down a street no wider than an alleyway, just ahead of me.

I didn't think crows were nocturnal, but then they're a confusing sort of animal at the best of times. Just consider all the superstitions associated with them. Good luck, bad luck— it's hard to work them all out.

Some say that seeing a crow heralds a death.

Some say a death brings crows so that they can ferry us on from this world to the next.

Some say it just means there's a change coming.

And then there's that old rhyme: One for sorrow, two for mirth...

It gets so you don't know what to think when you see one. But I do know it's definitely oh-so-odd to see them at this time of night. I can't help but follow in their wake. I don't even have to consider it; I just go, the quickened scuff of my boots not quite loud enough to envelop the sound of their wings.

The crows lead me through the winding streets, past the closed shops and cafés, past the houses with their hidden gardens and occasional walkways overhead that join separate buildings, one to the other, until we're deep in Old Market, following a steadily-narrowing lane that finally opens out onto a small town square.

I know this place. Christy used to come here and write sometimes, though I don't think he's done it for a while. And he's certainly not here tonight.

The square is surrounded on three sides by tall brick buildings leaning against each other, cobblestones underfoot. There's an old-fashioned streetlight in the center of the square with a wrought iron bench underneath, facing the river. On the far side of the river I can barely see Butler Common, the wooded hills beyond its lawns, and on the tops of the hills, a constellation of twinkling house lights.

By the bench is an overturned shopping cart with all sorts of junk spilling out of it. I can make out bundles of clothes, bottles and cans, plastic shopping bags filled with who knows what, but what holds my gaze is the man lying beside the cart. I've seen him before, cadging spare change, pushing that cart of his. He looks bigger than he probably is because of the layers of baggy clothes, though I remember him as being portly anyway. He's got a tuque on his head and he's wearing fingerless gloves and mismatched shoes. His hairline is receding, but he still has plenty of long, dirty-blond hair. His stubble is just this side of an actual beard, greyer than his hair. He's lying face-up, staring at the sky.

At first I think he's sleeping, then I think he's collapsed there. It's when I see the ghost that I realize he's dead.

The ghost is sitting on the edge of the cart—an insubstantial version of the prone figure, but this one is wearing a rough sort of armour instead of those layers of raggedy clothes. A boiled leather breastplate over a rough sort of tunic, leggings and leather boots. From his belt hangs an empty scabbard. Not big enough for a broadsword, but not small either.

I start forward, only I've forgotten the crows. The flap of

their descending wings draws my gaze up and then I can't hold on to the idea of the dead man and his ghost anymore, because somewhere between the moment of their final descent and landing, the pair changes from crows into girls.

They're not quite children, but they don't have adult physiques either. I'm just over five feet, but they're shorter and even slighter of build. Their skin is the colour of coffee with a dash of milk, their hair an unruly lawn of blue-black spikes, their faces triangular in shape with large green eyes and sharp features. I can't tell them apart and decide they must be twins, even dressing the same in black combat boots, black leggings and black oversized raggedy sweaters that seem to be made of feathers. They look, for all the world, like a pair of…

"Crow girls," I hear myself say in a voice that's barely a whisper.

I lower myself down onto the cobblestones and sit with my back against the brick wall of the house behind me. This is a piece of magic, one of those moments when the lines between what is and what might be blur like smudged charcoal. Pentimento: You can still see the shapes of the preliminary sketch, but now there are all sorts of other things hovering and crowding at the edges of what you initially drew.

I remember how I started thinking about superstitions when I first saw these two girls as crows. How there are so many odd tales and folk beliefs surrounding crows and other blackbirds: what seeing one, or two, or three might mean. I can't think of one that says anything about seeing them flying at night. Or what to do when you stumble upon a pair of them that can take human form and hold a conversation with a dead man....

One of the girls perches by the head of the corpse and begins to play with its hair, braiding it. The other sits cross-legged on the ground beside her twin and gives her attention to the ghost.

"I was a knight once," the ghost says.

"We remember," one of the girls tells him.

"I'm going to be a knight again."

The girl braiding the corpse's hair looks up at the ghost. "They might not have knights where you're going."

"Do you know that?"

"We don't know anything," the first girl says. She makes a steeple with her hands and looks at him above it. "We just are."

"Tell us about the King's Court again," her twin says.

The ghost gives a slow nod of his head. "It was the greatest court in all the land..."

I close my eyes and lean my head back against the wall of the building I'm sitting against, the bricks pulling at the tangles of my hair. The ghost's voice holds me spellbound and takes me back, in my mind's eye, to an older time.

"It was such a tall building, the tallest in all the land, and the King's chambers were at the very top. When you looked out the window, all creation lay before you."

I start out visualizing one of the office buildings downtown, but the more I listen, the less my mind's eye can hold the image. What starts out as a tall, modern office skyscraper slowly drifts apart into mist, reforms into a classic castle on top of a steep hill with a town spread out along the slopes at its base. At first I see it only from the outside, but then I begin to imagine a large room inside and I fill it with details. I see a hooded hawk on a perch by one window. Tapestries hang from the walls. A king sits on his throne at the head of a long table around which are numerous knights dressed the same as the ghost. The ghost is there, too. He's younger, taller, his back is straighter. Hounds lounge on the floor.

In Old Market, the dead man talks of tourneys and fairs, of border skirmishes and hunting for boar and pheasant in woods so old and deep we can't imagine their like anymore. And as he speaks, I can see those tourneys and country fairs, the knights and their ladies, small groups of armed men skirmishing in a moorland, the ghost saying farewell to his lady and riding into a forest with his hawk on his arm and his hound trotting beside his horse.

Still, I can't help but hear under the one story he tells, another story: one of cocktail parties and high-rise offices, stocks and mergers, of drops in the market and job losses, alcohol and divorce. He's managed to recast the tragedy of his life into a story from an old picture book. King Arthur. Prince Valiant. The man who lost his job, his wife and his family, who ended up dying, homeless and alone on the streets where he lived, is an errant knight in the story he tells.

I know this, but I can't see it. Like the crow girls, I'm swallowed by the fairy tale.

The dead man tells now of that day's hunting in the forests near the castle. How his horse is startled by an owl and rears back, throwing him into a steep crevice where he cracks his head on a stone outcrop. The hawk flies from his wrist as he falls, the laces of its hood catching on a branch and tugging it off. The hound comes down to investigate, licks his face, then lies down beside him.

When night falls, the horse and hound emerge from the forest. Alone. They approach the King's castle, the hawk flying overhead. And there, the ghost tells us, while his own corpse lies at the bottom of the crevice, his lady stands with another man's arm around her shoulders.

"And then," the ghost says, "the corbies came for their dinner and what baubles they could find."

I open my eyes and blink, startled for a moment to find myself still in Old Market. The scene before me hasn't changed. One of the crow girls has cut off the corpse's braid and now she's rummaging through the items spilled from the shopping cart.

"That's us," the other girl says. "We were the corbies. Did we eat you?

"What sort of baubles?" her companion wants to know. She holds up a Crackerjack ring that she's found among the litter of the ghost's belongings. "You mean like this?"

The ghost doesn't reply. He stands up and the crow girls scramble to their feet as well.

"It's time for me to go," he says.

"Can I have this?" the crow girl holding the Crackerjack ring asks.

The other girl looks at the ring that's now on her twin's finger. "Can I have one, too?"

The first girl hands her twin the braid of hair that she's cut from the corpse.

After his first decisive statement, the ghost now stands there looking lost.

"But I don't know where to go," he says.

The crow girls return their attention to him.

"We can show you," the one holding the braid tells him.

Her twin nods. "We've been there before."

I watch them as they each take one of his hands and walk with him toward the river. When they reach the low wall, the girls become crows again, flying on either side of the dead man's ghostly figure as he steps through the wall and continues to walk, up into the sky. For one long moment the impossible image holds, then they all disappear. Ghost, crow girls, all.

I sit there for a while longer before I finally manage to stand up and walk over to the shopping cart. I bend down and touch the corpse's throat, two fingers against the carotid artery, searching for a pulse. There isn't one.

I look around and see a face peering down at me from a second-floor window. It's an old woman, and I realize I saw her earlier, that she's been there all along. I walk toward her house and knock on the door.

It seems to take forever for anyone to answer, but finally a light comes on in the hall and door opens. The old woman I saw upstairs is standing there, looking at me.

"Do you have a phone?" I ask. "I need to call 911."

- 3 -

What a night it had been, Gerda thought.

She stood on her front steps with the rather self-contained

43

young woman who'd introduced herself as Jilly, not quite certain what to do, what was expected at a time such as this. At least the police had finally gone away, taking that poor homeless man's body with them, though they had left behind his shopping cart and the scatter of his belongings that had been strewn about it.

"I saw you watching from the window," Jilly said. "You saw it all, but you didn't say anything about the crow girls."

Gerda smiled. "Crow girls. I like that. It suits them."

"Why didn't you say anything?"

"I didn't think they'd believe me." She paused for a moment, then added, "Why don't you come in and have a cup of tea?"

"I'd like that."

Gerda knew that her kitchen was clean, but terribly old-fashioned. She didn't know what her guest would think of it. The wooden kitchen table and chairs were the same ones she and Jan had bought when they'd first moved in, more years past than she cared to remember. A drip had put a rusty stain on the porcelain of her sink that simply couldn't be cleaned. The stove and fridge were both circa 1950—bulky, with rounded corners. There was a long wooden counter along one wall with lots of cupboards and shelves above and below it, all laden with various kitchen accoutrements and knickknacks. The window over the sink was hung with lacy curtains, its sill a jungle of potted plants.

But Jilly seemed delighted by her surroundings. While Gerda started the makings for tea, putting the kettle on the stove, teacups on the table, Jilly got milk from the fridge and brought the sugar bowl to the table.

"Did you know him?" Gerda asked.

She took her Brown Betty teapot down from the shelf. It was rarely used anymore. With so few visitors, she usually made her tea in the cup now.

"The man who died," she added.

"Not personally. But I've seen him around on the streets. I think his name was Hamish. Or at least that's what people called him."

"The poor man."

Jilly nodded. "It's funny. You forget that everyone's got their own movie running through their heads. He'd pretty much hit rock bottom here in the world we all share, but the whole time, in his own mind he was living the life of a questing knight. Who's to say which was more real?"

When the water began to boil, Gerda poured a little into the teapot to warm it up. Emptying it into the sink, she dropped in a pair of teabags and filled the teapot, bringing it to the table to steep. She sat down across from her guest, smoothing down her skirt. The cats finally came in to have a look at the company, Swarte Meg first, slipping under the table and up onto Gerda's lap. The other two watched from the doorway.

"Did...we really see what I think we saw?" Gerda asked after a moment's hesitation.

Jilly smiled. "Crow girls and a ghost?"

"Yes. Were they real, or did we imagine them?"

"I'm not sure it's important to ask if they were real or not."

"Whyever not?" Gerda said. "It would be such a comfort to know for certain that some part of us goes on."

To know there was a chance one could be joined once more with those who had gone on before. But she left that unsaid.

Jilly leaned her elbow on the table, chin on her hand, and looked toward the window, but was obviously seeing beyond the plants and the view on the far side of the glass panes, her gaze drawn to something that lay in an unseen distance.

"I think we already know that," she finally said.

"I suppose."

Jilly returned her attention to Gerda.

"You know," she said. "I've seen those crow girls before, too—just as girls, not as crows—but I keep forgetting about them, the way the world forgets about people like Hamish." She sat up straighter. "Think how dull we'd believe the world to be without them to remind us…"

Gerda waited a moment, watching her guest's gaze take on that dreamy distant look once more.

"Remind us of what?" she asked after a moment.

Jilly smiled again. "That anything is possible."

Gerda thought about that. Her own gaze went to the window. Outside, she caught a glimpse of two crows flying across the city skyline. She stroked Swarte Meg's soft black fur and gave a slow nod. After what she had seen tonight, she could believe it, that anything was possible.

She remembered her husband Jan—not as he'd been in those last years when the illness had taken him, but before that. When they were still young. When they had just married and all the world and life lay ahead of them. That was how she wanted it to be when she finally joined him again.

If anything were possible, then that was how she would have it be.

THE BUFFALO MAN

The oaks were full of crows, as plentiful as leaves, more of the raucous black-winged birds than Jilly had ever seen together in one place. She kept glancing out the living room window at them, expecting some further marvel, though their enormous gathering was marvel enough all on its own. The leaded panes framed group after group of them in perfect compositions, which made her itch to draw them in the sketchbook she hadn't thought to bring along.

"There are an awful lot of crows out there this evening," she said after her hundredth inspection of them.

"You'll have to forgive her," the professor told their hosts with a smile. "Sometimes I think she's altogether too concerned with crows and what they're up to. For some people it's the stock market, others it's the weather. It's a fairly new preoccupation, but it does keep her off the streets."

"As if."

"Before this it was fruit faeries," the professor added, leaning forward from the sofa where he was sitting, his tone confidential.

"Wasn't."

The professor tched. "As good as was."

"Well, we all need a hobby," Cerin said.

"This is, of course, true," Jilly allowed, after first sticking out her tongue at the pair of them. "It's so sad that neither of you have one."

She'd been visiting with Professor Dapple, involved in a long, meandering conversation concerning Kickaha Mountain ballads vis-à-vis their relationship to British folktales, when he suddenly announced that he was due for tea at the Kelledys' that afternoon and did she care to join them? Was the Pope Catholic? Did the moon have wings? Well, one out of two wasn't bad, and of course she had to come.

The Kelledys' rambling house on Stanton Street was a place of endless fascination for her, with its old-fashioned architecture, all gables and gingerbread, with climbing vines and curious rooflines. The rooms were full of great solid pieces of furniture that crouched on Persian carpets and the hardwood floors like sleeping animals, not to mention any number of wonderfully bright and mysterious things perched on the shelves and sideboards, on the windowsills and meeting rails, like so many half-hidden lizards and birds. And then there were the oak trees that surrounded the building, a regular forest of them, larger and taller than anywhere else in the city, each one easily a hundred years old.

The house was magic in her eyes, as much as the couple who inhabited it, and she loved any excuse to come by for a visit. On a very lucky day, Cerin would bring out his harp, Meran her flute, and they would play a haunting, heart-lifting music that Jilly never heard except from them.

"I didn't know fruit had their own faeries," Meran said. "The trees, yes, but not the individual fruit itself."

"I wonder if there are such things as acorn faeries," Cerin said.

"I must ask my father."

Jilly gave a theatrical sigh. "We're having far too long a conversation about fruit and nuts, and whether or not they have faeries, and not nearly enough about great, huge, cryptic parliaments of crows."

"It would be a murder, actually," the professor put in.

"Whatever. I think it's wonderfully mysterious."

"At this time of the day," Meran said, "they'd be gathering together to return to their roosts."

Jilly shook her head. "I'm not so sure. But if that *is* the case, then they've decided to roost in your yard."

She turned back to look out over the leaf-covered lawn that lay under the trees, planning some witty observation that would make them see just how supremely marvelous it all was, but the words died unborn in her throat as she watched a large, bald-headed Buddha of a man step onto the Kelledys' walk. He was easily the largest human being she'd ever seen—she couldn't guess how many hundreds of pounds he must weigh—but oddly enough he moved with the supple grace of a dancer a fraction his size. His dark suit was obviously expensive and beautifully tailored, and his skin was as black as a raven's wing. As he came up the walk, the crows became agitated and flew around him, filling the air, their hoarse cries growing so loud that the noise resounded inside the house with the windows closed.

But neither the enormous man, nor the actions of the crows, was what had dried up the words in Jilly's throat. It was the limp figure of a slender man that the dapper Buddha carried in his arms. In sharp contrast, he was poorly dressed for the brisk weather, wearing only a raggedy shirt and jeans so worn they had almost no colour left in them. His face and arms were pale as alabaster; even his braided hair was white— yet another striking contrast to the man carrying him. She experienced something familiar yet strange when she gazed on his features, like taking out a favourite old sweater she hadn't worn in years, and feeling at once quite unacquainted with it and affectionately comfortable when she put it on.

"That's no crow," Cerin said, having stepped up to the window to stand beside Jilly's chair.

Meran joined him, then quickly went to the door to let the new visitor in. The professor rose from the sofa when she ushered the man and his burden into the room, waving a hand toward the seat he'd just quit.

"Put him down here," he said.

The black man nodded his thanks. Stepping gracefully across the room, he knelt and carefully laid the man out on the sofa.

"It's been a long time, Lucius," the professor said as the man straightened up. "You look different."

"I woke up."

"Just like that?"

Lucius gave him a slow smile. "No. A red-haired storyteller gave me a lecture about responsibility, and I realized she was right. It had been far too long since I'd assumed any."

He turned his attention to the Kelledys.

"I need a healing," he said.

There was something formal in the way he spoke the words, like a subject might speak to his ruler, though there was nothing remotely submissive in his manner.

"There are no debts between us," Cerin said.

"But now—"

"Nonsense," Meran told him. "We've never turned away someone in need of help before and we don't mean to start now. But you'll have to tell us how he was injured."

She knelt down on the floor beside the sofa as she spoke. Reaching out, she touched her middle finger to the center of his brow, then lifted her hand and moved it down his torso, her palm hovering about an inch above him.

"I know little more than you at this point," Lucius said.

"Do you at least know who he is?" Cerin asked.

Lucius shook his head. "The crow girls found him lying by a dumpster behind the Williamson Street Mall. They tried to heal him, but all they could manage was to keep him from slipping further away. Maida said he was laid low by ill will."

Jilly's ears perked up at the mention of the crow girls. They were the real reason for her current interest in all things corvid—a pair of punky, black-haired young women who seemed to have the ability to change your entire perception of the world simply by stepping into the periphery of your life. Ever since she'd first seen them in a café, she kept spotting them in the most unlikely places, hearing the most wonderful stories about them. Whenever she saw a crow now, she'd peer closely at it, wondering if this was one of the pair in avian form.

"That makes it more complicated," Meran said.

Sitting back on her heels, she glanced at Lucius. He gave her an apologetic look.

"I know he has buffalo blood," he told her.

"Yes, I see that."

"What did Maida mean by ill will?" Cerin asked. "He doesn't appear to have any obvious physical injuries."

Lucius shrugged. "You know how they can be. The more they tried to explain it to me, the less I understood."

Jilly had her own questions as she listened to them talk, such as why hadn't someone immediately called for an ambulance, or why had this Lucius brought the injured man here, rather than to a hospital? But there was a swaying, eddying sensation in the air, a feeling that the world had turned a step from the one everyone knew and they now had half a foot in some other, perhaps more perilous, realm. She decided to be prudent for a change and listen until she understood better what was going on.

She wasn't the only one puzzled, it seemed.

"We need to know more," Meran said.

Lucius nodded. "I'll see if I can find them."

"I'll come with you," Cerin said.

Lucius hesitated for a long moment, then gave another

nod and the two men left the house. Jilly half expected them to fly away, but when she looked out the window she saw them walking under the oaks toward the street like an ordinary, if rather mismatched, pair, Lucius so broad and large that the tall harper at his side appeared slender to the point of skinniness. The crows remained in the trees this time, studying the progress of the two men until they were lost from sight.

"I have some things to fetch," Meran said. "Remedies to try. Will you watch over our patient until I get back?"

Jilly glanced at the professor.

"Um, sure," she said.

And then the two of them were alone with the mysteriously stricken man. Laid low by ill will. What did *that* mean?

Jilly pulled a footstool over to the sofa where Meran had been kneeling and sat down. Looking at the man, she found herself wishing for pencil and sketchbook again. He was so handsome, like a figure from a Pre-Raphaelite painting. Except for the braids and raggedy clothes, of course. Then she felt guilty for where her thoughts had taken her. Here was the poor man, half dead on the sofa, and all she could think about was drawing him.

"He doesn't look very happy, does he?" she said.

"Not very."

"Where do you know Lucius from?"

The professor took off his wire-rimmed glasses and gave them a polish they didn't need before replacing them.

"I can't remember where or when I first met him," he said. "But it was a long time ago—before the war, certainly.

55

Not long after that he became somewhat of a recluse. At first I'd go visit him at his house—he lives just down the street from here—but then it came to the point where he grew so withdrawn that one might as well have been visiting a sideboard or a chair. Finally I stopped going 'round."

"What happened to him, do you think?"

The professor shrugged. "Hard to tell with someone like him."

"You're being deliberately mysterious, aren't you?"

"Not at all. There just isn't much to say. I know he's related to the crow girls. Their grandfather, or an uncle or something. I never did quite find out which."

"So that's why all the crows are out there."

"I doubt it," the professor said. "He's corbae, all right, but raven, not crow."

Jilly felt a thrill of excitement. A raven uncle, crow girls, the man on the sofa with his buffalo blood. She was in the middle of some magical story for once, rather than on the edges of it looking in, and her proximity made everything feel bright and clear and very much in focus. Then she felt guilty again because it had taken someone getting hurt to draw her into this story. Considering the unfortunate circumstances, it didn't seem right to be so excited by it.

She turned back to look at the pale man lying there so still.

"I wonder if he can turn into a buffalo," she said.

"I believe it's more of a metaphorical designation," the professor told her, "rather than an actual shape-shifting option."

Jilly shook her head. She could remember the night in Old Market when she'd first seen the crow girls slip from crow to girl and back again. It wasn't exactly something you forgot, though oddly enough, the memory did have a tendency to try to slip away from her. To make sure it didn't, she'd fixed the moment in pigment and hung the finished painting on the wall of her studio as a reminder.

"I don't think so," she said. "I think it's a piece of real magic."

She leaned closer to the man and reached forward to push aside a few long white hairs that had come to lie across his lashes. When she touched him, that swaying, eddying sensation returned, stronger than ever. She had long enough to say, "Oh, my," then the world slipped away and she was somewhere else entirely.

- 2 -

"I *have* resumed my responsibilities," Lucius said as the two men walked to his house a few blocks farther down Stanton Street.

Cerin gave him a sidelong glance. "Guilt's a terrible thing, isn't it?"

"What do you mean?"

The harper shrugged. "It makes you question people's motives, even when they're as straightforward as my wanting to help you find a pair of somewhat wayward and certainly mischievous relatives."

"They can be a handful," Lucius said. "It's possible we'll

57

find them more quickly with your help."

Cerin hid a smile. He knew that was about as much of an apology as he'd be getting, but he didn't mind. He hadn't really wanted one. He'd only wanted Lucius to understand that no one was holding him to blame for withdrawing from the world the way he had—at least no one in the Kelledy household was. Responsibility was a sharp-edged sword that sometimes cut too deep, even for an old spirit such as Lucius Portsmouth.

So all he said was, "Um-hmm," then added, "Odd winter we've been having, isn't it? So close to Christmas and still no snow. I wonder whose fault *that* is."

Lucius sighed. "You can be insufferable."

This time Cerin didn't hide his smile. "As Jilly would say, it's just this gift I have."

"But I appreciate your confidence."

"Apology accepted," Cerin told him, unable to resist.

"You wouldn't have any crow blood in you, would you?"

"Nary a drop."

Lucius harrumphed and muttered, "I'd still like to see the results of a DNA test."

"What was that?"

"I said, I wonder where they keep their nest."

Stanton Street was lined with oaks, not so old as those that grew around the Kelledy house, but they were stately monarchs nonetheless. Having reached the Rookery where Lucius lived, the two men paused to look up where the bare branches of the trees laid their pattern against the sky above. Twilight had given way to night and they could see stars peeking down from amongst the boughs. Stars, but no black-haired, giggling crow girls. Lucius called, his voice ringing up into the trees like a raven's cry.

Kaark. Kaark. Tok.

There was no reply.

"They weren't so happy with this foundling of theirs," Lucius said, turning to his companion. "At first I thought it was because their healing didn't take, but when I carried him to your house, I began to understand their uneasiness."

He called again, but there was still no response.

"What do you find so troubling about him?" Cerin asked.

Though he had an idea. There were people and places that were like doors to other realms, to the spiritworld and to worlds deeper and older than that. In their presence, you could feel the world shift uneasily underfoot, the ties binding you to it loosening their grip—an unsettling sensation for anyone, but more so for those who could normally control where they walked.

The still, pale man with his white braids had been like that.

Lucius said as much, then added, "The trouble with such doors isn't so much what they open into, as what they can close you from."

Cerin nodded. To be denied access to the spiritworld would be like losing a sense. One's hearing, one's taste.

"So you don't think they'll come," he said.

Lucius shrugged. "They can be willful...not so responsible as some."

"Let me try."

59

"Never let it be said I turned down someone's help."

Cerin smiled. He closed his eyes and reached back to his home, back to a room on the second floor. A harp stood there with a rose carved into the wood where curving neck met forepillar. His fingers twitched at his sides and the sound of that roseharp was suddenly in the air all around them, a calling-on song that rose up as though from the ground and spun itself out against the branches above, then higher still, as though reaching for the stars.

"A good trick," Lucius said. "Cousin Brandon does much the same with his instrument, though in his case, he's the only one to hear its tones."

"Perhaps you're not listening hard enough," Cerin said.

"Perhaps."

He might have said more, but there came a rustling in the boughs above them and what appeared to be two small girls were suddenly there, hanging upside down from the lowest branch by their hooked knees, laughter crinkling in the corners of their eyes while they tried to look solemn.

"Oh, that was veryvery mean," Maida said.

Zia gave an upside down nod. "Calling us with magic music."

"We'd give you a good bang on the ear."

"Reallyreally we would."

"Except the music's so pretty."

"Ever so truly pretty."

"And magic, of course."

Cerin let the harping fall silent.

"We need you to tell us more about the man you found,"

60

he said.

The crow girls exchanged glances.

"Surely such wise and clever people as you don't need help from us," Maida said.

"That would be all too very silly," Zia agreed.

"And yet we do," Cerin told them. "Will you help us?"

There was another exchange of glances between the pair, then they dropped lightly to the ground.

"Are there sweets in your house?" Zia asked.

"Mountains of them."

"Oh, good," Maida said. She gave Lucius a sad look. "Old Raven never has any sweets for us."

Zia nodded. "It's veryvery sad. What kind do you have?"

"I'm not sure."

"Well, come on," Maida said, taking Cerin's hand. "We'd better hurry up and find out."

Zia nodded, looking a little anxious. "Before someone else eats them all."

In this mood, Cerin didn't know that they'd get anything useful out of the pair, but at least they'd agreed to come. He'd let Meran sort out how to handle them once he got them home.

Zia took his other hand and with the pair of them tugging on his hands, they started back up Stanton Street. Lucius took the rear, a smile on his face as the crow girls chattered away to Cerin about exactly what their favourite sweets were.

Jilly was no stranger to the impossible, so she wasn't as surprised as some might have been to find herself transported from the Kelledys' living room, full of friendly shadows and known corners, to an alleyway that could have been anywhere. Still, she wasn't entirely immune to the surprise of it all and couldn't ignore the vague, unsettled feeling that was tiptoeing up and down the length of her spine.

Because that was the thing about the impossible, wasn't it? When you did experience it, well, first of all, hello, it proved to be all too possible, and secondly, it made you rethink all sorts of things that you'd blindly agreed to up to this point. Things like the world being round—was gravity really so clever that it kept people on the upside down part of the world from falling off into the sky? That Elvis was dead—if he was, then why did *so* many people still see him? That UFOs were actually weather balloons or swamp gas—never mind the improbability of so many balloons going AWOL, how did a swamp get indigestion in the first place?

So being somewhere she shouldn't be didn't render Jilly helpless, stunned, or much more than curiously surprised. By looking up at the skyline, she placed herself in an alleyway behind the Williamson Street Mall, right where the crow girls had found—

Her gaze dropped to the mound of litter beside the closest dumpster, and there he was, Meran's comatose patient, except here, in this wherever she was, he was sitting on top of the garbage, knees drawn up to his chin, and regarding her with a gloomy gaze. She focused on the startling green of his eyes. Odd, she thought. Weren't albinos supposed to have red, or at least pink, eyes?

She waited a moment to give him the opportunity to speak first. When he didn't, she cleared her throat.

"Hello," she said. "Did you bring me here?"

He frowned at the question. "I don't know you, do I?"

"Well, we haven't been formally introduced or anything, and while you weren't exactly the life of the party when I first met you, right now we're sharing the same space somewhere else, as well as here, which is sort of like us knowing each other, or at least me knowing you."

He gave her a confused look.

"Oh, that's right. You wouldn't remember, being unconscious and all. I'm not sure of all the details myself, but you're supposed to have been, and I quote, 'laid low by ill will,' and when I went to brush some hair out of your eyes, I found myself here, with you again, except you're awake this time. How were you laid low by this ill will? I'm assuming someone hit you, which would be ill will-ish enough so far as I can see, but somehow I think it's more than that."

She paused and gave him a rueful smile. "I guess I'm not doing a very good job with this explanation, am I?"

"How can you be so cheerful?" he asked her.

Jilly pulled a battered wooden fruit crate over to where he was sitting and sat down herself.

"What do you mean?" she asked.

"The world is a terrible place," he said. "Every day, every moment, its tragedies deepen, the mean-spiritedness of its

63

inhabitants quickens and escalates until one can't imagine a kindness existing anywhere for more than an instant before being suffocated."

"Well, it's not perfect," Jilly agreed. "But that doesn't mean we have to—"

"I can see that you've been hurt and disappointed by it— cruelly so, when you were much younger. Yet here you sit before me, relatively trusting, certainly cheerful, optimism bubbling in you like a fountain. How can this be?"

Jilly was about to make some lighthearted response, speaking without thinking as she did too often, but then part of what he'd said really registered.

"How would you know what my life was like when I was a kid?"

He shrugged. "Our histories are written on our skin— how can you be surprised that I wouldn't know?"

"It's not something I've ever heard of before."

"Perhaps you have to know how to look for the stories."

Well, that made a certain kind of sense, Jilly thought. There were so many hidden things in the world that only came into focus when you learned how to pay attention to them, so why not stories on people's skin?

"So," she said. "I guess nobody could lie to you, could they?"

"Why do you think the world depresses me the way it does?"

"Except it's not all bad. You can't tell me that the only stories people have are bad ones."

"They certainly outweigh the good."

"Maybe *you're* not looking in the right place."

"I understand thinking the best of people," he said. "Looking for the good in them, rather than the wrongs they've done. But ignoring the wrongs is almost like condoning them, don't you think?"

"I don't ignore them," Jilly told him. "But I don't dwell on them either."

"Even when you've been hurt as much as you have?"

"Maybe especially because of that," she said. "What I try to do is make people feel better. It's hard to be mean when you're smiling, or when a laugh's building up inside of you."

"That's a child's view of the world."

Jilly shook her head. "A child lives in the now, and they're usually pretty self-absorbed. Which is what can make them unaware of other people's feelings at times."

"I meant simplistic."

Jilly wouldn't accept that, either. "I'm aware of what's wrong. I just try to balance it with something good. I know I can't solve every problem in the world, but if I try to help the ones I come upon as I go along, I think it makes a difference. And you know, most people aren't really bad. They're just kind of thoughtless at times."

"How can you believe that? Listen to them and then tell me again how they're really kind at heart."

Jilly's head suddenly filled with conversation.

…why do I have to buy anything for that old bag, anyway…

…hello, can't we leave the kids at home for one afternoon…the miserable, squalling monsters…

…hear that damn song one more time, I'll kill…

65

No, they were thoughts, she realized, stolen from the shoppers in the mall that lay on the other side of the alley's wall. It was impossible to tell their age or gender except by inference.

...damn bells...oh, it's the Sally Ann, doing their annual beg-a-thon...hey, nice rack on her...wonder why a looker like her's collecting money for losers...

...doesn't get me what I want this year, I'll show him what being miserable is all about...

Jilly blinked when the voices were suddenly gone again.

"Now do you see?" her companion said.

"Those thoughts are taken out of context with the rest of their lives," Jilly told him. "Just because someone has an ugly thought, it doesn't make them a bad person."

"Oh no?"

"And being kind oneself does make a difference."

"Against the great swell of indifferent unkindnesses that threaten to wash us completely away with the force of a tsunami?"

"Is this what they meant with the ill will that laid you low?"

"What who meant?"

"The crow girls. They're the ones who found you and brought you to the Kelledys' house because they couldn't heal you themselves."

A small smile touched his features. "I remember some crow girls I saw once. Their good humour could make yours seem like grumbling, but they carried the capacity for large angers, as well."

66

"Was that when you were a buffalo?"

"What do you know about buffalo?"

"You're supposed to have buffalo blood," Jilly explained.

He gave her a slow nod.

"Those-who-came," he said. "They slaughtered the buffalo. Then, when the People danced and called the buffalo spirit back, they slaughtered the People, as well. That's the history I read on the skin of the world—not only here, but everywhere. Blood and pain and hunger and hatred. It's an old story that has no end. How can a smile, a laugh, a good deed, stand up against the weight of such a history?"

"I…I guess it can't," Jilly said. "But you still have to try."

"Why?"

"Because that's all you can do. If you don't try to stand up against the darkness, it swallows you up."

"And if in the end, there is only darkness? If the world is meant to end in darkness?"

Jilly shook her head. She refused to believe it.

"How can you deny it?" he asked.

"It's just…if there's only supposed to be darkness, then why were we given light?"

For a long moment, he sat there, shoulders drooped, staring down at his hands. When he finally looked up, there was something in his eyes that Jilly couldn't read.

"Why indeed?" he said softly.

- 4 -

When Meran returned to the living room it was to find Jilly

67

slumped across the body of her patient, Professor Dapple standing over the pair of them, hands fluttering nervously in front of him.

"What's happened?" she said, quickly crossing the room.

"I don't know. One moment she was talking to me, then she leaned over and touched his cheek and she simply collapsed."

He moved aside as Meran knelt down by the sofa once more. Before she could study the problem more closely, the roseharp began to play upstairs.

The professor looked surprised, his gaze lifting to the ceiling.

"I thought Cerin had gone with Lucius," he said.

"He did," Meran told him. "That's only his harp playing."

The professor regarded her for a long, slow moment.

"Of course," he finally said.

Meran smiled. "It's nothing to be nervous about. Really. I'm more worried about what's happened to Jilly."

The sofa was wide enough that, with the professor's help, she was able to lay Jilly out beside the stranger. Whatever had struck Jilly down was as much of a mystery to Meran as the stranger's original ailment. In her mind she began to run through a list of other healers she could contact to ask for help when there was a sudden commotion at the front door. A moment later the crow girls trooped in with Cerin and Lucius following behind them.

"Jilly...?" Cerin began.

Meran briefly explained what little she knew of what had

happened since they'd been gone.

"We can't help him," Zia said before anyone else could speak.

"We tried," Maida added, "but we weren't so very useful, were we?"

Zia shook her head.

"Not very useful at all," Maida said.

"But," Zia offered, "we could maybe help her."

Maida nodded and leaned closer to peer at Jilly. "She's very pretty, isn't she? I think we know her."

"She's Geordie's friend," Zia said.

"Oh, yes." Zia looked at Cerin. "But he plays much nicer music."

"Ever so very much more."

"It's for listening to, you see. Not for making you do things."

"I'm sorry," Cerin said. "But we needed to get your attention."

"Well, we're ever so very attentive now," Maida told him.

Whereupon the pair of them went very still and fixed Cerin with expectant gazes. He turned helplessly to his wife.

"How can you help Jilly?" she asked.

"Jilly," Maida repeated. "Is that her name?"

"Silly Jilly."

"Willy-nilly."

"Up down dilly."

"I'm sure making fun of her name's helpful," Lucius said.

"Oh, pooh," Maida said. "Old Raven never gets a joke."

"That's the trouble with this raven, all right," Zia agreed.

"We've seen jokes fly right out the window when they see he's in the room."

"About Jilly," Meran tried again.

"Well, you see," Maida said, suddenly serious. "The buffalo man is a piece of the Grace."

"And we can't help the Grace—she has to help herself."

Maida nodded. "But Jilly—"

Zia giggled, then quickly put a hand over her mouth.

"—only needs to be shown the way back to her being all of one piece again," Maida finished.

"You mean her spirit has gone somewhere?" Cerin asked.

"Duh."

"How can we bring her back?" Meran asked.

The crow girls looked at Cerin.

"Well," Zia said. "If you know her calling-on song as well as you do ours, that would maybe work."

"I'll get the roseharp," Cerin said, standing up.

"Now he needs it in hand," Lucius said.

Cerin started to frame a reply, but then he looked at Meran and left the room.

"We were promised sweets," Maida said.

Zia nodded. "The actual promise was that there'd be mountains of them."

"Do you mind if we finish up here first?" Meran asked.

"Oh, no," Maida said. "We love to wait."

Zia gave Meran a bright smile. "Honestly."

"Anticipation is so much better than being attentive."

"Though they're much the same, in some ways."

"Because they both involve waiting, you see," Maida

explained, her smile as bright as her companion's.

Meran stifled a sigh and returned their smile. She'd forgotten how maddening the crow girls could be. Normally she enjoyed bantering with their tricksy kind, but at the moment she was too worried about Jilly to join the fun. And then there was the stranger whose appearance had started it all. They hadn't even *begun* to deal with him.

When Cerin returned with the roseharp, he sat down on a footstool and drew the instrument onto his lap.

"Play something Jilly," Maida suggested.

"Did you say silly?" Zia asked. "Because that's not being serious at all, you know, making jokes about very serious things."

"I didn't say silly."

"I think maybe you did."

Cerin ignored the pair of them and turned to his wife. "I might not be able to bring her back," he said. "Because of him. Because of the doors he can close."

"I know," Meran said. "You can only try."

- 5 -

"I think I know now what the crow girls meant," Jilly said.

The buffalo man raised his eyebrows questioningly.

"About this ill will business," Jilly explained. "Every ugly thought or bad deed you come into contact with steals away a piece of your vitality, doesn't it? It's like erosion. The pieces keep falling away until finally you get so worn away that you slip into a kind of coma."

71

"Something like that."

"Has this happened before?"

He nodded.

"So what happens next?"

"I die."

Jilly stared at him, not sure she'd heard him right.

"You...die."

He nodded. "And then I come back and the cycle begins all over again."

Neither of them spoke for a long moment then. It was quiet in the alley where they sat, but Jilly could hear the traffic go by down the block where the alley opened on to the street. There was a repetitive pattern to the sound: bus, bus, a car horn, a number of vehicles in a group, then the buses again.

"I guess what I don't understand," Jilly finally said, "is why all the good things in the world don't balance it out—you know, recharge your vitality."

"They're completely overshadowed," he said.

Jilly shook her head. "I don't believe that. I know there are awful things in the world, but I also know there's more that's good."

"Then why am I so weak right now, in this, your season of goodwill?"

"I think it's because you don't let the good in anymore. You don't trust there to be any good left, so you've put up these protective walls that keep it out."

"And the bad? Why does it continue to affect me?"

"Because you concentrate on it," Jilly said. "And by doing that, you let it get in. It's like you're doing the exact opposite

72

to what you should be doing."

"If only it could be so simple."

"But it is," she said. "In the end, it always comes down to small, simple things because that's the way the world really works. We're the ones who make it so complicated. I mean, think about it. If everybody really and truly treated each other the way they'd want to be treated, all the problems of the world would be solved. Nobody would starve, because nobody'd want to go hungry themselves. Nobody would steal, or kill, or hurt each other, because they wouldn't want that to happen to themselves."

"So what stops them from doing so?" he asked.

"Trust. Or rather a lack of it. Too many people don't trust the other person to treat them right, so they just dig in, accumulating stuff, thinking only of themselves or their own small group—you know, family, company, community, whatever. A tribal thing." She hesitated a moment, then added, "And that's what's holding you back, too. You don't trust the good to outweigh the bad."

"I don't know that I even can."

"No one can help you with that," Jilly told him. "That's something that can only come from inside you."

He gave her a slow nod. "Maybe I will try harder, the next time."

"What next time? What's wrong with right now?"

He held out his arms. "If you could read the history written on my skin, you would not need to ask that question."

Jilly pushed up her sleeves and held out her own arms.

"Look," she said. "You read what I went through as a kid.

I'm no better or stronger or braver than you are. But I am determined to leave things a little better than they were before I got here. That's what gets me through. And I have to admit there's a certain selfishness involved. You see, I want to live in that better world. I know it's not going to happen unless we all clean up our act and I know I can't make anybody else do that. But I'll be damned if I don't do it myself. You know, like a Kickaha friend of mine says, 'live large and walk in Beauty.'"

"You are very…persuasive."

Jilly grinned. "It's just this gift I have."

She stood up and offered him a hand.

"So what do you say, buffalo man? You want to give this life another shot?"

He allowed her to help him up to his feet.

"There's a problem," he said.

"No, no, no. Ignore the negatives, if only for now."

"You don't understand. The door that brought us here— it only opens one way."

"What door?"

"My old life was finished and I was on my way to the new. All of this—" He made a motion with his hand to encompass everything around them. "—is only a memory."

"Whose memory?" Jilly asked, getting a bad feeling.

"Mine. The memory of a dying man."

She smiled brightly. "So live. I thought we'd already been through this earlier."

"I would. You've convinced me enough of that. Only there's no way back."

"There's always a way back…isn't there?"

He didn't answer. He didn't have to.

"Oh, great. I get to be in a magical adventure, only it turns out to be like a train on a one-way track and we left the happy ending station miles back."

"I'm sorry."

She took his hand and gave it a squeeze. "Me too."

- 6 -

"Nothing's happening," Maida said.

Zia peered at the two still bodies on the sofa. She gave Jilly a gentle poke with her finger.

"She's still veryvery far away," she agreed.

Cerin sighed and let his fingers fall from the strings of the roseharp. The music echoed on for a few moments, then all was still.

"I tried to put all the things she loves into the calling-on," he said. "Painting and friendship and crows and whimsy, but it's not working. Wherever she's gone, it's farther than I can reach."

"How did it happen anyway?" the professor asked. "All she did was touch him. Meran did the same and she wasn't taken away."

"Jilly's too open and trusting," Meran said. "She didn't think to guard herself from the man's spirit. When we fall away into death, most of us will grab hold of anything we can to stay our fall. That's what happened to her—he grabbed her and held on hard."

"He's dying?"

75

Meran glanced at the professor and nodded.

"I should never have brought him here," Lucius said.

"You couldn't have known."

"It's our fault," Zia said.

Maida nodded glumly. "Oh, we're the most miserably bad girls, we are."

"Let's worry about whose fault it was some other time," Meran said. "Right now I want to concentrate on where he could have taken her."

"I've never died," Lucius said, "so I can't say where a dying man would draw another's soul, but I've withdrawn from the world…"

"And?" Meran prompted him.

"I went into my own mind. I lived in my memories. I didn't *remember*. I lived in them."

"So if we knew who he was," Cerin said. "Then perhaps we could—"

"We don't need to know who he is," Meran broke in. "All we need to know is what he was thinking."

"Would the proverbial life flashing before one's eyes be relevant here?" the professor asked. "Because that could touch on anything."

"We need something more specific," Cerin said.

Meran nodded. "Such as…where the crow girls found him. Wouldn't he be thinking of his surroundings at some point?"

"It's still a one-way door," Cerin pointed out.

"But if we can open it even a crack…" Lucius said.

Cerin smiled. "Then maybe we can pull them out before

it closes on us again."

"We can do that," Maida said.

Zia nodded. "We're very good at opening things."

"Even better when there's sweets inside."

Zia rapped on the man's head with a knuckle.

"Hello, hello in there," she said. "Can you hear me?"

"Zia!" Lucius said.

"Well, how else am I supposed to get his attention?"

"Hold on," Meran said. "Perhaps we're going about this all wrong. Instead of concentrating on the door he is, we should be concentrating on the door Jilly is."

"Oh, good idea," Maida said.

The crow girls immediately turned their attention to Jilly. They leaned close, one on either side, and began whispering in her ears.

- 7 -

"So I guess this is sort of like a recording," Jilly said, "except instead of being on pause, we're in a tape loop."

Which was why the traffic noise she heard was so repetitive. Being part of his memory, it, too, was in a loop.

"You have such an interesting way of looking at things," the buffalo man said.

"No, humour me in this. We're in a loop of your memory, right? Well, what's to stop you from thinking of something else? Or concentrating and getting us past the loop?"

"To what purpose?"

"To whatever comes next."

"We know what comes next," he said.

"No. You *assume* we do. The last thing you seem to remember is lying here in this alleyway. You must have passed out at that point, which is the loop we're in. Except I showed up and you're conscious and we've been talking—none of this is memory. We're already somewhere else than your memory. So what's to stop you from taking us further?"

"I have no memory beyond the point where I closed my eyes."

But Jilly was on a roll.

"Of course not," she said. "So we'll have to use our imaginations."

"And imagine what?"

"Well, crows would be good for starters. The crow girls would have been flying above, and then they noticed you and…" She paused, cocking her head. "Listen. Can you hear that?"

At first he shook his head, but then his gaze lifted and the strip of sky above the alley went dark with crows. A cloud of them blocked the sun, circling just above the rooftops and filling the air with their raucous cries.

"Wow," Jilly said. "You've got a great imagination."

"This isn't my doing," he said.

They watched as two of the birds left the flock and came spiraling down on their black wings. Just before they reached the pavement, they changed into a pair of girls with spiky black hair and big grins.

"Hello, hello!" they cried.

"Hello, yourselves," Jilly said.

She couldn't help but grin back at them.

"We've come to take you home," one of them said.

"You can't say no."

"Everyone will think it's our fault if you don't come."

"And then we won't get any sweets."

"Not that we're doing this for sweets."

"No, we're just very kindhearted girls, we are."

"Ask anyone."

"Except for Raven."

They were tugging on her hands now, each holding one of hers with two of their own.

"Don't dawdle," the one on her right said.

Jilly looked back at the buffalo man.

"Go on," he said.

She shook her head. "Don't be silly."

For some reason that made the crow girls giggle.

"There's no reason you can't come too," she said. She turned to look at the crow girls. "There isn't, is there?"

"Well..." one of them said.

"I suppose not."

"The door's closed," the buffalo man told them. "I can feel it inside, shut tight."

"Your door's closed," one of the girls agreed.

"But hers is still open."

Still he hesitated. Jilly pulled away from the crow girls and walked over to him.

"Half the trick to living large," she said, "is the living part."

He let her take him by the hand and walk him back to where the crow girls waited. Holding hands, with one of the spiky-haired girls on either side of them, they walked toward the mouth of the alleyway. But before they could get halfway there…

* * *

Jilly blinked and opened her eyes to a ring of concerned faces.

"We did it, we did it, we did it!" the crow girls cried.

They jumped up from Jilly's side and danced around in a circle, banging into furniture, stepping on toes and generally raising more of a hullabaloo than would seem possible for two such small figures. It lasted only a moment before Lucius put a hand on each of their shoulders and held them firmly in place.

"And very clever you were, too," he said as they squirmed in his grip. "We're most grateful."

Jilly turned to look at the man lying next to her on the sofa.

"How are you feeling?" she asked.

His gaze made a slow survey of the room, taking in the Kelledys, the professor, Lucius and the wriggling crow girls.

"Confused," he said finally. "But in a good way."

The two of them sat up.

"So you'll stay?" Jilly asked. "You'll see it through this time?"

"You're giving me a choice?"

Jilly grinned. "Not likely."

Long after midnight, the Kelledys sat in their living room looking out at the dark expanse of their lawn. The crows were still roosting in the oaks, quiet now except for the odd rustle of feathers or a soft, querulous croak. Lucius and the crow girls had gone back down the street to the Rookery, but not before the two girls had happily consumed more cookies, chocolates and soda pop than seemed humanly possible. But then, they weren't human, they were corbae. The professor and Jilly had returned to their respective homes as well, leaving only a preoccupied buffalo man who'd finally fallen asleep in one of the extra rooms upstairs.

"Only a few more days until Christmas," Cerin said.

"Mmm."

"And still no snow."

"Mmm."

"I'm thinking of adopting the crow girls."

Meran gave him a sharp look.

He smiled. "Just seeing if you were paying attention. What were you thinking of?"

"If there's a word for a thing because it happens, or if it happens because there's a word for it."

"I'm not sure I'm following you."

Meran shrugged. "Life, death. Good, bad. Kind, cruel. What was the world like before we had language?"

"Mercurial, I'd think. Like the crow girls. One thing would flow into another. Nothing would have been really separate from anything else because everything would have been made up of pieces of everything else."

"It's like that now."

Cerin nodded. "Except we don't think of it that way. We have the words to say this is one thing, this is another."

"So we've lost…what? A kind of harmony?"

"Perhaps. But we gained free will."

Meran sighed. "Why did we have to give up the one to gain the other?"

"I don't know for sure, but I'd guess it's because we need to be individuals. Without our differences, without our needing to communicate with one another, we'd lose our ability to create art, to love, to dream…"

"To hate. To destroy."

"But most of us strive for harmony. The fact that we can fall into the darkness is what makes our choice to reach for the light such a precious thing."

Meran leaned her head on his shoulder.

"When did you become so wise?" she asked.

"When you chose me to be your companion on your journey into the light."

A CROW GIRLS' CHRISTMAS
(with MaryAnn Harris)

"We have jobs," Maida told Jilly when she and Zia dropped by the professor's house for a visit at the end of November.

Zia nodded happily. "Yes, we've become veryvery respectable."

Jilly had to laugh. "I can't imagine either of you ever being completely respectable."

That comment drew an exaggerated pout from each of the crow girls, the one more pronounced than the other.

"Not being completely respectable's a good thing," Jilly assured them.

"Yes, well, easy for you to say," Zia said. "You don't have a cranky uncle always asking when you're going to do something useful for a change."

Maida nodded. "You just get to wheel around and around in your chair and not worry about all the very serious things that we do."

"Such as?" Jilly asked.

Zia shrugged. "Why *don't* pigs fly?"

"Or why is white a colour?" Maida offered.

"Or black."

"Or yellow ochre."

"Yellow ochre is a colour," Jilly said. "Two colours, actually. And white and black are colours, too. Though I suppose they're not very *colourful*, are they?"

"Could it be more puzzling?" Zia asked.

Maida simply smiled and held out her teacup. "May I have a refill, please?"

Jilly pushed the sugar bag over to her. Maida filled her teacup to the brim with sugar. After a glance at Zia, she filled Zia's cup as well.

"Would you like some?" she asked Jilly.

"No, I'm quite full. Besides, too much tea makes me have to pee."

The crow girls giggled.

"So what sort of jobs did you get?" Jilly asked.

Zia lowered her teacup and licked the sugar from her upper lip.

"We're elves!" she said.

Maida nodded happily. "At the mall. We get to help out Santa."

"Not the *real* Santa," Zia explained.

"No, no. He's much too very busy making toys at the North Pole."

"This is sort of a cloned Santa."

"Every mall has one, you know."

"And *we*," Zia announced proudly, "are in charge of handing out the candy canes."

"Oh my," Jilly said, thinking of the havoc that could cause.

"Which makes us very important," Maida said.

"Not to mention useful."

"So pooh to Lucius, who thinks we're not."

"Do they have lots of candy canes in stock?" Jilly asked.

"Mountains," Zia assured her.

"Besides," Maida added. "It's all magic, isn't it? Santa never runs out of candy or toys."

That was before you were put in charge of the candy canes, Jilly thought, but she kept her worry to herself.

* * *

Much to everyone's surprise, the crow girls made excellent elves. They began their first daily four-hour shift on December 1, dressed in matching red-and-green outfits that the mall provided: long-sleeved jerseys, short pleated skirts, tights, shoes with exaggerated curling toes, and droopy elf hats with their rowdy black hair poking out from underneath. There were bells on their shoes, bells at the end of their hats, and they each wore brooches made of bells that they'd borrowed from one of the stores in the mall. Because they found it next to impossible to stand still for more than a few seconds at a time, the area around Santa's chair echoed with their constant jingling.

Parents waiting in line, not to mention their eager children, were completely enchanted by their happy antics and the ready smiles on their small dark faces.

"I thought they'd last fifteen minutes," their uncle Lucius confided to the professor a few days after the pair had started, "but they've surprised me."

"I don't see why," the professor said. "It seems to me that they'd be perfectly suited for the job. They're about as elfish as you can get without being an elf."

"But they're normally so easily distracted."

The professor nodded. "However, there's candy involved, isn't there? Jilly tells me that they've been put in charge of the candy canes."

"And isn't that a source for pride." Lucius shook his head and smiled. "Trust them to find a way to combine sweets with work."

"They'll be the Easter Bunny's helpers in the spring."

Lucius laughed. "Maybe I can apprentice them to the Tooth Fairy."

The crow girls really were perfectly suited to their job. Unlike many of the tired shoppers that trudged by Santa's chair, they remained enthralled with every aspect of their new environment. The flashing lights. Jingling bells. Glittering tinsel. Piped-in Christmas music. Shining ornaments.

And, of course, the great abundance of candy canes.

They treated each child's questions and excitement as though that child were the first to have this experience. They talked to those waiting in line, made faces so that the children would laugh happily as they were having their pictures taken, handed out candy canes when the children were lifted down from Santa's lap. They paid rapt attention to every wish expressed, and adored hearing about all the wonderful toys available in the shops.

Some children, normally shy about a visit to Santa, returned again and again, completely smitten with the pair.

But mostly, it was all about the candy canes.

The crow girls were extremely generous in handing them out, and equally enthusiastic about their own consumption. They stopped themselves from eating as many as they might have liked, but did consume one little candy cane each for every five minutes they were on the job.

Santa, busy with the children, and also enamoured with his cheerful helpers, failed to notice that the sacks of candy canes in the storage area behind his chair were dwindling at an astonishing rate. He never thought to look because it had never been an issue before. There'd always been plenty of candy canes to go around in past years.

* * *

On December 19, at the beginning of their noon shift, there were already lines and lines of children waiting excitedly to visit Santa and his crow girl elves. As the photographer was unhooking the cord to let the children in, Maida turned to Zia to ask where the next sack of candy canes was just as Zia asked Maida the very same question. Santa suggested that they'd better hurry up and grab another sack from the storage space.

Trailing the sound of jingling bells, the crow girls went behind his chair.

Zia pulled aside the little curtain.

"Oh-oh," she said.

Maida pushed in beside her to have a look herself. The two girls exchanged worried looks.

"They're all gone," Zia told Santa.

"I'll go to the stockroom for more," Maida offered.

Zia nodded. "Me too."

"What stockroom?" Santa began, but then he realized exactly what they were saying. His normally rosy cheeks went as white as his whiskers.

"They're all gone?" he asked. "*All* those bags of candy canes?"

"In a word, yes."

"But where could they all have gone?"

"We give them away," Maida reminded him. "Remember?"

Zia nodded. "We were supposed to."

"So that's what we did."

"Because it's our job."

"And we ate a few," Maida admitted.

"A veryvery few."

Santa frowned. "How many is a few?"

"Hmm," Zia said.

"Good question."

"Let's see."

They both began to count on their fingers as they talked.

"We were veryvery careful not to eat more than twelve an hour."

"Oh so very careful."

"So in four hours—"

88

"—that would be forty-eight—"

"—times two—"

"—because there are two of us."

They paused for a moment, as though to ascertain that there really were only two of them.

"So that would be…um…"

"Ninety-six—"

"—times how many days?"

"Eighteen—"

"—not counting today—"

"—because there aren't any today—"

"—which is why we need to go the stockroom to get more."

Santa was adding it all up himself. "That's almost two thousand candy canes you've eaten!"

"Well, almost," Maida said.

"One thousand, seven hundred and twenty-eight," Zia said.

"If you're keeping count."

"Which is *almost* two thousand, I suppose, but not really."

"Where *is* the candy cane stockroom?" Maida asked.

"There isn't one," Santa told her.

"But—"

"And that means," he added, "that all the children here today won't get any candy canes."

The crow girls looked horrified.

"That means us, too," Zia said.

Maida nodded. "We'll also suffer, you know."

"But we're ever so stoic."

"Ask anybody."

"We'll hardly complain."

"And never where you can hear us."

"Except for now, of course."

Santa buried his face in hands, completely disconcerting the parent approaching his chair, child in hand.

"Don't worry!" Maida cried.

"We have everything under control." Zia looked at Maida. "We do, don't we?"

Maida closed her eyes for a long moment, then opened them wide and grinned.

"Free tinsel for everyone!" she cried.

"I don't want tinsel," the little boy standing in front of Santa with his mother said. "I want a candy cane."

"Oh, you do want tinsel," Maida assured him.

"Why does he want tinsel?" Zia asked.

"Because...because..."

Maida grabbed two handfuls from the boughs of Santa's Christmas tree. Fluttering the tinsel with both hands over her head, she ran around the small enclosure that housed Santa's chair.

"Because it's so fluttery!" she cried.

Zia immediately understood. "And shiny!" Grinning, she grabbed handfuls of her own.

"Veryvery shiny," Maida agreed.

"And almost as good as candy," Zia assured the little boy as she handed him some. "Though not quite as sugary good."

The little boy took the tinsel with a doubtful look, but then Zia whirled him about in a sudden impromptu dance.

Soon he was laughing and waving his tinsel as well. From the line, all the children began to clap.

"We want tinsel, too!" one of them cried.

"Tinsel, tinsel!"

The crow girls got through their shift with great success. They danced and twirled on the spot and did mad acrobatics. They fluttered tinsel, blew kisses, jingled their bells, and told stories so outrageous that no one believed them, but everyone laughed.

By the end of their shift, even Santa had come around to seeing "the great excellent especially good fortune of free tinsel."

Unfortunately, the mall management wasn't so easily appeased and the crow girls left the employ of the Williamson Street Mall that very day, after first having to turn in their red-and-green elf outfits. But on the plus side, they were paid for their nineteen days of work and spent all their money on chocolate and fudge and candy and ice cream.

When they finally toddled out of the mall into the snowy night, they made chubby snow angels on any lawn they could find, all the way back to the Rookery.

* * *

"So now we're unemployed," Zia told Jilly when they came over for a visit on the twenty-third, shouting "Happy eve before Christmas Eve!" as they trooped into the professor's house.

"I heard," Jilly said.

"It was awful," Maida said.

Jilly nodded. "Losing a job's never fun."

"No, no, no," Zia said. "They ran out of candy canes!"

"Can you imagine?" Maida asked.

Zia shook her head. "Barely. And I was there."

"Well, I'm sorry to hear that," Jilly said.

"Yes, it's a veryvery sorrysome state of affairs," Maida said.

"And we're unemployed, too!"

"Lucius says we're unemployable."

"Because now we have a record."

"A permanent record."

"Of being bad bad candy cane-eating girls."

They both looked so serious and sad that Jilly became worried. But then Zia laughed. And Maida laughed, too.

"What's so funny?" Jilly asked.

Zia started to answer, but she collapsed in giggles and couldn't speak.

Maida giggled, too, but she managed to say, "We sort of like being bad bad candy cane-eating girls."

Zia got her fit of giggles under control. "Because it's like being outlaws."

"Fierce candy cane-eating outlaw girls."

"And that's a good thing?" Jilly asked.

"What do you think?" Maida asked.

"I think it is. Merry Christmas, Maida. Merry Christmas, Zia."

"Merry Christmas to you!" they both cried.

Zia looked at Maida. "Why did you say, 'Merry Christmas toot toot'?"

"I didn't say 'toot toot'."

"I think maybe you did."

"Didn't."

Zia grinned. "Toot toot!"

"Toot toot!"

They pulled their jingling bell brooches out of their pockets, which they'd forgotten to return to the store where they'd "found" them, and marched around the kitchen singing "Jingle Bells" at the top of their lungs until Goon, the professor's housekeeper, came in and made them stop.

Then they sat at the table with their cups of sugar, on their best behaviour, which meant they only took their brooches out every few moments, jingled them, and said "toot toot" very quietly. Then giggling, they'd put the brooches away again.

MAKE A JOYFUL NOISE

Everyone thinks we're sisters, but it's not as simple as that. If I let my thoughts drift far enough back into the long ago—the *long* long ago, before Raven stirred that old pot of his and poured out the stew of the world—we were there. The two of us. Separate, but so much the same that I suppose we could have been sisters. But neither of us remembers parents, and don't you need them to be siblings? So what exactly our relationship is, I don't know. We've never known. We just *are*. Two little mysteries that remain unchanged while the world changes all around us.

But that doesn't stop everyone from thinking they know us. In the Kickaha tradition, we're the tricksters of their crow story cycles, but we're not really tricksters. We don't play tricks. Unless our trick is to look like we'd play tricks, and then we don't.

Before the Kickaha, the cousins had stories about us, too,

though they were only gossip. Cousins don't buy into mythic archetypes because we all know how easy it is to have one attached to your name. Just ask Raven. Or Cody.

But gossip, stories, anecdotes...everybody seems to have something to pass along when it comes to us.

These days it's people like Christy Riddell who tell the stories. He puts us in his books, the way his mentor Professor Dapple used to do, except Christy's books are actually popular. I suppose we don't mind so much. It's kind of fun to be in a story that anyone can read. But if we have to have a Riddell brother in our lives, we'd much prefer it to be Geordie. There's nothing wrong with Christy. It's just that he's always been a bit stiff. Geordie's the one who knows how to have fun and that's why we get along with him so well, because we certainly like to have fun.

But we're not only about mad gallivanting and cartwheels and sugar.

And we're not some single entity, either.

That's another thing that people get wrong. They see the two of us as halves of one thing. Most of the time they don't even recognize us when they meet us on our own. Apart, we're just like anybody else, except we live in trees and can change into birds. But when you put the two of us together, everything changes. We get all giddy and incoherence rules. It's like our being near each other causes a sudden chemical imbalance in our systems and it's almost impossible to be anything but silly.

We don't particularly mind being that way, but it does make people think they know just who and what and why we are, and they're wrong. Well, they're not wrong when the two of us are together. They're just wrong for who we are when we're on our own.

And then there are the people who only see us as who *they* want us to be, rather than who we really are—though that happens to everybody, I suppose. We all carry around other people's expectations of who we are, and sometimes we end up growing into those expectations.

* * *

It was a spring day, late in the season, so the oaks were filled with fresh green foliage, the gardens blooming with colour and scent, and most days the weather was balmy. Today was no exception. The sun shone in a gloriously blue sky and we were all out taking in the weather. Zia and I lounged on the roof of the coach house behind the Rookery, black-winged cousins perched in the trees all around us, and up on the roof of the Rookery we could see Lucius's girlfriend Chlöe standing on the peak, staring off into the distance. That meant that Lucius was deep in his books again. Whenever he got lost in their pages, Chlöe came up on the roof and did her wind-vane impression. She was very good at it.

"What are you looking at?" we asked her one day.

It took her a moment to focus on us and our question.

"I'm watching a wren build a nest," she finally said.

"Where?" Zia asked, standing on her tiptoes and trying to see.

"There," Chlöe said and pointed, "in that hedge on the edge of Dartmoor."

Neither of us was ever particularly good with geography, but even we knew that at least half a continent and an ocean lay between us and Dartmoor.

"Um, right," I said.

Other times she said she was watching ice melt in Greenland. Or bees swarming a new queen above a clover field somewhere in Florida. Or a tawny frogmouth sleeping in an Australian rainforest.

After a while we stopped asking. And we certainly didn't fly over and ask her what she was looking at today. We were too busy lounging—which is harder to do on a sloped roof than you might think—until Zia suddenly sat up.

"I," she announced, "have an astonishingly good idea."

I'd just gotten my lounging position down to an absolute perfection of casualness, so I only lifted a questioning eyebrow.

"We should open a store," she said.

"Selling what?"

"That's just it. It will be a store where people bring us things and we put them in the store."

"And when it gets all filled up?"

She grinned. "Then we open another. We just keeping doing it until we have an empire of stores, all across the country."

"We don't have the money to buy anything," I said.

She nodded. "That's why they'd have to just give us the stuff. We'll be like a thrift shop, except we wouldn't sell anything we got."

"That seems greedy. What do we need with things?"

"We can give everything away once we've established our empire. It's just for fun."

"It seems more like a lot of work."

She sighed and shook her head. "You are so veryvery lazy."

"That's because today is a day especially made for being lazy."

"No, today's a day for building an empire of stores and if you won't help, I'll do it myself."

"I'll help later."

She nodded. "When all the hard work will probably be done."

"That's the risk I'll have to take."

She stuck her tongue out at me, then shifted to bird shape and a black crow went winging off above the oaks that line Stanton Street. I laid my head on the shingles again and went back to my very successful lounging.

I was so good at it that, eventually, I fell asleep.

* * *

When I woke, it was dark. Chlöe was still standing on the peak of the Rookery, and the trees around me were now filled with sleeping black birds. Above, the sky held a wealth of stars only slightly dimmed by the city's pollution. I looked for Zia. She wasn't back yet, so I slid down to the edge of the roof and dropped the remaining distance onto the dew-damp lawn. Cousins stirred in the trees at the soft thump of my landing on the grass, but went back to sleep when they saw it was only me.

I left the grounds of the Rookery and walked along Stanton Street heading for downtown, where I supposed I'd find Zia. I wondered if she'd actually had any success getting her silly plan off the ground, or if she'd gotten distracted after leaving me and was now up to who knew what sort of mischief.

I could understand her getting distracted—it's such an easy thing to have happen. For instance, there were so many interesting houses and apartments on either side of the street as I continued to walk through Lower Crowsea. It was late enough that most of them were dark, but here and there I found lit windows. They were like paintings in an enormous art gallery, each offering small and incomplete views into their owners' lives.

Zia and I like to visit in people's houses when they're sleeping. We slip in and walk through the empty rooms, helping ourselves to sweets or fruit, if they're the sort of people to leave them out in small welcoming bowls or baskets. There might as well be a sign that says, "Help yourself."

But we really don't take much else when we go inside. A bauble here, some unwanted trinket there. Mostly we just wander from room to room, looking, looking, looking. There are whole stories in the placement of vases and knickknacks, in what pictures and paintings have been hung, where, and in what order. So we admire the stories on the walls and windowsills, the shelves and mantles. Or we sit at a desk, a dining room table, or on the sofa, leafing through a scrapbook, a school yearbook, a magazine that's important to whoever home this is.

We're curious, yes, but not really all that snoopy, for all that it might seem the exact opposite. We're only chasing the ghosts and echoes of lives that we could never have.

So, as I continued past Stanton Street, I forgot that I was looking for Zia. My gaze went up the side of an apartment building that rose tall above me and I chose a unit at random.

Moments later I was inside, taking in the old lady smells: potpourri, dust and medicine. I stood quietly for a moment, then began to explore.

* * *

"Maddy?" an old woman's voice called from a room down the hall.

It was close enough to my name to make me sit up in surprise. I put down the scrapbook I'd been looking at and walked down the short hall, past the bathroom, until I was standing in the doorway of a bedroom.

"Is that you, Maddy?" the old woman in the bed asked.

She was sitting up, peering at me with eyes that obviously couldn't see much, if anything.

I didn't have to ask her who Maddy was. I'd seen the clippings from the newspaper pasted into the scrapbook. She'd been the athletic daughter, winning prize after prize for swimming and gymnastics and music. The scrapbook was about half full. The early pages held articles clipped from community and city newspapers, illustrated with pictures of a happy child growing into a happy young woman over the years, always holding trophies, smiling at the camera.

She wasn't in the last picture. That photo was of a car crumpled up against the side of an apartment building, under a headline that read, "Drunk Driver Kills Redding High Student." The date on the clipping was over thirty years old.

"Come sit with Mama," the old lady said.

I crossed the room and sat cross-legged on the bed. When she reached out her hand, I let her take mine. I closed my fingers around hers, careful not to squeeze too hard.

"I've missed you so much," she said.

She went on, but I soon stopped listening. It was much more interesting to look at her because, even though she was sitting up and talking, her eyes open as though she were awake, I realized that she was actually still asleep.

Humans can do this.

They can talk in their sleep. They can go walking right out of their houses, sometimes. They can do all sorts of things and never remember it in the morning.

Zia and I once spent days watching a woman who was convinced she had fairies in her house cleaning everything up after she'd gone to bed. Except she was the one who got up in her sleep and tidied and cleaned before slipping back under the covers. To show her appreciation to the fairies, she left a saucer of cream on the back steps—which the local cats certainly appreciated—along with biscuits or cookies or pieces of cake. We ate those on the nights we came by, but we didn't help her with her cleaning. That would make us bad fairies, I suppose, except for the fact that we weren't fairies at all.

After a while the old woman holding my hand stopped talking and lay back down again. I let go of her hand and tucked it under the covers.

It was a funny room that she slept in. It was full of memories, but none of them were new or very happy. They made the room feel musty and empty even though she used it every day. It made me wonder why people hung on to memories if they just made them sad.

I leaned over and kissed her brow, then got off the bed.

When I came back to the living room, there was the ghost

of a boy around fifteen or sixteen sitting on the sofa where I'd been looking through the old lady's scrapbook earlier. He was still gawky, all arms and legs, with features that seemed too large at the moment, but would become handsome when he grew into them. Except, being a ghost, he never would.

Under his watchful gaze, I stepped up onto the coffee table and sat cross-legged in front of him.

"Who are you?" I asked.

He seemed surprised that I could see him, but made a quick recovery.

"Nobody important," he said. "I'm just the other child."

"The other…"

"Oh, don't worry. You didn't miss anything. I'm the one that's not in the scrapbooks."

There didn't seem much I could add to that, so I simply said, "I don't usually talk to ghosts."

"Why not?"

I shrugged. "You're not usually substantial enough, for one thing."

"That's true. Normally, people can't even see me, never mind talk to me."

"And for another," I went on, "you're usually way too focused on past wrongs and the like to be any fun."

He didn't argue the point.

"Well, I know why I'm here," he said, "haunting the place I died and all that. But what are you doing here?"

"I like visiting in other people's houses. I like looking at their lives and seeing how they might fit if they were mine."

I looked down at the scrapbook on the coffee table.

"So you were brother and sister?" I asked.

He nodded.

"Does she ever come back here?"

He laughed, but without any mirth. "Are you kidding? She hated this place. Why do you think she joined any school club and sports team that would have her? She'd do anything to get out of the house. Mother kept her on such a tight leash that she couldn't fart without first asking for permission."

"But you're here."

"Like I said, I died here. In my own room. I got stung by a bee that came in through the window. No one knew I was allergic. My throat swelled up and I asphyxiated before I could try to get any help."

"It sounds horrible."

"It was. They came back from one of Madeline's games and found me sprawled dead on the floor in my bedroom. It did warrant a small notice in the paper—I guess it was a slow news day—but that clipping never made it into a scrapbook."

"And now you're here…"

"Until she finally notices me," he finished for me.

"Why did she ignore you?" I asked. "When you were alive, I mean."

"I don't know. Madeline said it's because I looked too much like our dad. We were in grade school when he walked out on her, leaving her with a mess of debts and the two of us. I guess her way of getting over it was to ignore me and focus on Madeline, who took after her side of the family."

"Humans are so complicated," I said.

"Which you're not."

"Oh, I'm very complicated."

"I meant human."

"What makes you say that?" I asked.

He kept count on his fingers. "One, you can see me, which most people can't. Two, you can talk to me, which most people really can't. Three, you're sitting there all calm and composed, when most people—most *human* people—would be flipping out."

I shrugged. "Does it matter what I am?"

"Not really."

He looked down the hall as though he could see through the walls to where his mother lay sleeping. The mother who'd ignored him when he was alive and, now that he was dead, still ignored him. Her mind might be filled with old memories, but none were of him.

"Can you help me?" he asked.

"Help you with what?"

"With…you know. Getting her to remember me."

"Why is it so important?"

"How can I die and go on if no one remembers that I was ever alive?"

"Lots of people don't remember me," I said, "and it doesn't bother me."

He chuckled, but without any humour. "Yeah, like that's possible."

"No, it really doesn't."

"I meant that anybody would forget meeting you."

"You'd be surprised."

He held my gaze for a long moment, then shrugged.

"So will you help me?"

I nodded. "I can try. Maybe it's not so much that your mother should remember you more, but that she should remember your sister less. The way it seems, there's no room inside her for anything else."

"But you'll try?"

Against my better judgment, I found myself nodding.

He did a slow fade and I was left alone in the living room. I sat for a while longer, looking at the place where he'd been sitting, then slid off the coffee table and walked back into the hall. There were two closed doors and two open ones. I knew that one led into the old lady's bedroom, the other into a bathroom. I went to the first closed door. It opened into a room that was like stepping inside a cake, all frosty pinks and whites, full of dolls and pennants and trophies. Madeline's room. Closing its door, I continued down the hall and opened the other one.

Both rooms had the feel of empty places where no one lived. But while Madeline's room was bright and clean—the bed neatly made, shelves dusted, trophies shined—the boy's room looked as though the door had been shut on the day he died and no one had opened it until I had just this moment.

The bedding lay half-on, half-off the box spring, pooling on the floor. There were posters of baseball players and World War II planes on the wall. Decades of dust covered every surface, clustering around the model cars and plastic statues of movie monsters on the bookshelves and windowsill. More planes hung from the ceiling, held in flight by fishing lines strung with cobwebs.

Unlike the daughter, he truly was forgotten.

I walked to the desk where a half-finished model lay covered in dust. Books were stacked on the far corner with a school notebook on top. I cleared the dust with a finger and read the handwritten name on the "Property of" line:

Donald Quinn.

I thought of bees and drunk drivers, of being remembered and forgotten. I knew enough about humans to know that you couldn't change their minds. You couldn't make them remember if they didn't want to.

Why had I said I'd help him?

Among the cousins, a promise was sacred. Now I was committed to an impossible task.

I closed the door to the boy's room and left the apartment.

The night air felt cool and fresh on my skin, and the sporadic sound of traffic was welcome after the unhappy stillness of the apartment. I looked up at its dark windows, then changed my shape. Crow wings took me back to the Rookery on Stanton Street.

* * *

I think Raven likes us better when we visit him on our own. The way we explode with foolishness whenever Zia and I are together wears him down—you can see the exasperation in his eyes. He's so serious that it's fun to get him going. But I also like meeting with him one-on-one. The best thing is, he never asks me where Zia is. He treats us as individuals.

"Lucius," I said the next morning. "Can a person die from a bee sting?"

I'd come into his library in the Rookery to find him crouched on his knees, peering at the titles of books on a lower shelf. He looked up at my voice, then stood, moving with a dancer's grace that always surprises people who've made assumptions based on his enormous bulk. His bald head gleamed in the sunlight streaming in through the window behind him.

"What sort of a person?" he asked. "Cousin or human?"

"What's the difference?"

He shrugged. "Humans can die of pretty much anything."

"What do you mean?"

"Well, take tobacco. The smoke builds up tar in their lungs and the next thing you know, they're dead."

"Cousins smoke. Just look at Joe, or Whiskey Jack."

"It's not the same for us."

"Well, what about the Kickaha? They smoke."

He nodded. "But so long as they keep to ceremonial use, it doesn't kill them. It only hurts them when they smoke for no reason at all, rather than to respect the sacred directions."

"And bee stings?"

"If you're allergic—and humans can be allergic to pretty much anything—then, yes. It can kill them. Why do you ask?"

I shrugged. "I met a boy who died of a bee sting."

"A dead boy," Lucius said slowly, as though waiting for a punch line.

"I meant to say a ghost."

"Ah. Of course."

"He's not very happy."

Lucius nodded. "Ghosts rarely are." He paused a moment,

then added, "You didn't offer to help him, did you?"

He didn't wait for my reply. I suppose he could already see it in my face.

"Oh, Maida," he said. "Humans can be hard enough to satisfy, but ghosts are almost impossible."

"I thought they just needed closure," I said.

"Closure for the living and the dead can be two very different things. Does he want revenge on the bee? Because unless it was a cousin, it would be long dead."

"No, he just wants to be remembered."

Lucius gave a slow shake of his head. "You could be bound to this promise forever."

"I know," I said.

But it was too late now.

* * *

After leaving the Rookery, I flew up into a tree—not one of the old oaks on the property, but one farther down the street where I could get a little privacy as I tried to figure out what to do next. Like most corbae, I think better on a roost or in the air. I knew just trying to talk to Donald's mother wouldn't be enough. At some point, I'd have to, but first I thought I'd try to find out more about what exactly had happened to her children.

That made me cheer up a little because I realized it would be like having a case and looking into the background of it, the way a detective would. I'd be like a private eye in one of those old movies the Aunts liked to watch late at night when everybody else was asleep except for Zia and me. And probably Lucius.

I decided to start with the deaths and work my way back from them.

There was no point in trying to find the bee. As Lucius had said, unless it was a cousin, it would be long dead by now, and it didn't make sense that it would be a cousin. I could look into it, I supposed, but first I'd try to find the driver of the car that had struck Madeline. A bee wouldn't even be alive after thirty years, anyway. But a human might.

* * *

Most people know there are two worlds: the one Raven made and the otherworld, where dreams and spirits live. But there's another world that separates the two: the between. Thin as a veil in some places, wide as the widest sea in others. When you know the way, it's easy to slip from one to another, and that's what I do when I find myself standing in front of the locked door of Michael Clark's house. It's how Zia and I always get into places.

Slip into the between, take a step, then slip right back into Raven's world. It's as though you passed right through the door, except what you really did was take another, slightly more roundabout route.

I didn't like it in Clark's house when I got there that evening. There was an air of…unpleasantness about the place. I don't mean that it smelled bad, though there was a faint smell of mustiness and old body odour in the air. It was more that this was a place where not a lot of happiness had ever lived. Because places hold on to strong emotions just the way people do. The man who doesn't forgive? The house he lives in doesn't either. The house full of happy, laughing children? You

110

can feel its smile envelop you when you step through the door.

Clark's name had been in that last clipping in the old lady's scrapbook. When I looked it up in the telephone book, I found three listings for Michael Clark. The first two belonged to people much too young to be the man I was looking for, but this house…I knew as soon as I slipped inside that I was in the right place.

The front hall was messy with a few months' worth of flyers and old newspapers piled up against the walls, the kitchen garbage overflowing with take-out food containers and pizza boxes, the sink full of dirty mugs and other dishes. But there weren't any empty liquor bottles or beer cases full of empties.

I found Clark sitting on the sofa in his living room, watching the TV with the sound off. As with the rest of the place, this room was also a mess. Coming into it was like stepping onto a beach where the tide had left behind a busy debris of more food containers, newspapers, magazines, dirty clothes. A solitary, long-dead plant stood withered and dry in its pot on the windowsill.

Clark looked up when I came in and didn't even seem surprised to see me. That happens almost as often as it doesn't. Zia and I can walk into someone's kitchen while they're having breakfast, and all they do is take down a couple of more bowls from the cupboard and push the cereal box over to us. Or they'll simply move over a little to give us room on the sofa they're sitting on.

In Clark's case, he might have thought that I was another one of those personal demons he was obviously wrestling with on a regular basis.

I didn't bother with any small talk.

"It's not like they made it out to be," the man said, when I asked him about the night his car had struck Madeline. "I didn't try to kill her. And I wasn't drunk. I'd had a few beers, but I wasn't drunk. She just stepped out from behind a van, right in front of my car. She didn't even look. It was like she wanted to die."

"I've heard people do that," I said. "It seems so odd."

"I suppose. But there are times I can understand all too well. I lost everything because of that night. My business. My family. And that girl lost her life. *I* took her life."

There was more of that. A lot more.

When I realized I wasn't learning anything here except how to get depressed, I left him, still talking, only to himself. I looked up at the night sky, then took wing and headed for the scene of the accident that Michael Clark kept so fresh in his mind.

Between my ghost boy's mother and Michael Clark, I was beginning to see that the dead weren't the only ones haunted by the past.

* * *

The place where Madeline had died didn't look much different from any other part of the inner city. It had been so long since the accident, how could there be any sign that it had ever happened? But I thought, if her brother's ghost was still haunting the bedroom where he'd died, then perhaps she hadn't gone on yet either.

I walked along the sidewalk and down an alleyway,

calling. "Hello, hello! Hello, hello!"

I did it, over and over again, until a man wrenched open one of the windows overlooking the alley. I looked up into his angry features, though with the light of the window behind him, he was more just a shadow face.

"It's three o'clock in the morning!" he yelled. "Are you going to shut up, or do I have to come down there and shut you up?"

"You'll have to come down," I called back, "because I can't stop."

"Why the hell not?"

"I need to find a dead girl. Have you seen her?"

"Oh, for Christ's sake."

His head disappeared back into the apartment and he slammed the window shut. I went back to calling for Madeline until I heard footsteps behind me. I turned, warm with success, but it was only the grumpy man from the window. He stood in the mouth of the alley, peering down its length to where I stood.

He was older than I'd thought when I'd seen him earlier—late fifties, early sixties—and though he carried more weight than he probably should, he seemed fit. If nothing else, he smelled good, which meant he at least ate well. I hate the smell of people who only eat fast food. All that grease from the deep-frying just seems to ooze out of their pores.

"What's this about a dead girl?" he asked.

I pointed to the street behind him. "She got hit by a drunk driver just out there."

"You're not answering my question."

"I just want to talk to her," I told him. "To see how she feels."

"You just said she was dead. I don't think she's feeling much of anything anymore."

"Okay. How her *ghost* feels."

He studied me for a long moment, then that thing happened that's always happening around Zia and me: He just took me at my word.

"I don't remember anybody dying around here," he said. "At least not recently."

"It was thirty years ago."

"Thirty years ago…"

I could see his mind turning inward, rolling back the years. He gave me a slow nod.

"I do remember now," he said. "I haven't thought about it in a long time." He turned from me and looked out at the street. "This was a good neighbourhood, and it still is, but it was different back then. We didn't know about things so much. People drank and drove because they didn't know any better. A policeman might pull you over, but then if it looked like you could drive, he'd give you a warning and tell you to be careful getting home."

He nodded and his gaze came back to me. "I remember seeing the guy that killed that poor girl. He didn't seem that drunk, but he was sure shook up bad."

"But you didn't see the accident itself?"

He shook his head. "We heard it—my Emily and me. She's gone now."

"Where did she go?"

"I mean she's dead. The cancer took her. Lung cancer. See, that's another of those things. Emily never smoked, but she worked for thirty years in a diner. It was all that secondhand smoke that killed her. But we didn't know about secondhand smoke back then."

I didn't know quite what to say, so I didn't say anything. I don't think he even noticed.

"Now they're putting hormones in our food," he said, "and putting God knows what kind of animal genes into our corn and tomatoes and all. Who knows what that'll mean for us, ten, twenty years down the road?"

"Something bad?" I tried.

"Well, it won't be good," he said. "It never is." He looked down the alley behind me. "Are you going to keep yelling for this ghost to come talk to you?"

"I guess not. I don't think she's here anymore."

"Good," he said. "I may not work anymore, but I still like to get my sleep." He started to turn, then added, "Good luck with whatever it is you're trying to do."

And then he did leave and walked back down the street.

I watched him step into the doorway of his apartment, listened to the door hiss shut behind him. A car went by on the street. I went back into the alley and looked around, but I didn't call out because I knew now that nobody was going to hear me. Nobody dead, anyway.

I felt useless as I started back to the mouth of the alley. This had been a stupid idea and I still had to help the dead boy, but I didn't know how, or where to begin. I felt like I didn't know anything.

"What are you doing?" someone asked.

I looked up to see Zia sitting on the metal fire escape above me.

"I'm investigating."

"Whatever for?"

I shrugged. "It's like I'm a detective."

"More like you're nosy."

I couldn't help but smile, because it was true. But it wasn't a big smile, and it didn't last long.

"That, too," I said.

"Can I help?"

I thought of how that could go, of how quickly we'd dissolve into silliness and then forget what it was we were supposed to be doing.

"I'll be veryvery useful," she said, as though reading my mind. "You'll be in charge and I'll be your Girl Thursday."

"I think it's Girl Friday."

"I don't think so. Today's Thursday. *Tomorrow* I can be Girl Friday."

I gave her another shrug. "It doesn't matter. It turns out I'm a terrible detective."

She slid down the banister and plonked herself on the bottom step.

"Tell me about it," she said.

"It started out when I went looking for you and your store, but then I got distracted..."

* * *

"And now I feel like I'm forgetting what it's like to be happy," I said, finishing up. "It's like that stupid ghost boy stole all my happiness away, and now, ever since I talked to him, all I meet are unhappy people with very good reasons to be unhappy, and that makes me wonder, how could I ever have been happy? And what is being happy, anyway?"

Zia gave a glum nod. "I think it might be catching, because now I'm feeling the same way."

"You see? That's just what I mean. Why is it so easy to spread sadness and so hard to spread happiness?"

"I guess," Zia said, "because there's so much more sadness."

"Or maybe," I said, "it's that there's so much of it that nobody can do anything about."

"But we can do something about this, can't we?"

"What could we possibly do?

"Make the mother remember."

I shook my head. "Humans are very good at not remembering," I said. "It might be impossible for her to remember him now. She might not even remember him when she's dead herself and her whole life goes by in front of her eyes."

"Supposedly."

"Well, yes. If you're going to get precise, nobody knows if that's what really happens. But if it did, she probably wouldn't remember."

"And you can't just kill her to find out," Zia said.

"Of course not." I sighed. "So what am I going to do? I promised Donald I'd help him, but there's nothing I can do."

"I have an idea," Zia said, a mischievous gleam in her eye.

"This is serious—" I began, but she laid a finger across my

lips.

"I know. So we're going to be serious. But we're also going to make her remember."

"How?"

Zia grinned. "That's easy."

She stood up and slapped a hand against her chest.

"I," she announced, "am going to be a ghost."

I had a bad feeling, but nevertheless, I let her lead me back to the apartment that Donald's mother was haunting as much as he was, and she wasn't even dead.

* * *

Zia practiced making spooky noises the whole way back to the ghost boy's apartment, which didn't inspire any confidence in me, but once we were outside the building, she turned serious again.

"Is she alone in the apartment?" she asked.

"There's the ghost boy."

"I know. But is there anybody in there to look after her? You made it sound like she'd need help to take care of herself."

"I don't know," I said. "There was no one else there last night. I suppose somebody could come by during the day."

"Well, let's go see."

We flew up to the fire escape outside her kitchen window, lost our wings and feathers, and then stepped into the between. A moment later we were standing inside the kitchen. I could only sense the old woman's presence—at least hers was the only presence I could sense that was alive.

"Oh, Ghost Boy," Zia called in a loud whisper. "Come out, come out, wherever you are. If you come out, I have a nice little…" She gave me a poke in the shoulder. "What do ghosts like?"

"How should I know?"

She nodded, then called out again. "I have a nice little piece of ghost cake for you, if you'll just come out now."

Donald materialized in the kitchen by walking through a wall. He pointed a finger at Zia.

"Who's she?" he asked.

Zia looked at me.

"You didn't say he was so rude," she said before turning back to Donald. "I'm right here, you know. You could ask me."

"You look like sisters."

"And yet, we're not."

He ignored her, continuing to talk to me. "Is she here to help?"

"There, he's doing it again," Zia said.

"This is Zia," I said. "And Zia, this is Donald."

"I prefer Ghost Boy," she said.

"Well, it's not my name."

"She's here to help," I said.

"Really? So far, all she's been is rude and making promises she can't keep."

Zia bristled at that. "What sort of promises can't I keep?"

He shrugged. "For starters, I'm here, but where's my cake?"

They held each other's gaze for a long moment, and it was hard to tell which of them was more annoyed with the other. Then Zia's cheek twitched, and Donald's lips started to curve upward, and they were both laughing. Of course, that set me off too, and soon all three of us were giggling and snickering, Zia and I with our hands over our mouths so that we wouldn't wake Ghost Boy's mother.

Donald was the first to recover, but his serious features only set us off again.

"Okay," he said. "It wasn't *that* funny. So why are you still laughing?"

"Because we can," Zia told him.

"Because we can-can!" I added.

Then Zia and I put our arms around each other's waist and began to prance about the kitchen like Moulin Rouge can-can dancers, kicking our legs up high in unison. It was funny until my toe caught the edge of the table, which jolted a mug full of spoons, knocking it over and sending silverware clattering all over the floor.

Zia and I stopped dead and we all three cocked our heads.

Sure enough, a querulous cry came from down the hall.

"Who's out there?" the old woman called. "Is there somebody out there?"

That was followed a moment later by the sound of her getting out of her bed and slowly shuffling down the hall toward us. Long moments later, she was in the doorway and the overhead light came on, a bright yellowy glare that sent the shadows scurrying.

Zia and I had stepped into the between where we could see without being seen, but Donald stayed where he was, leaning against the kitchen counter, his arms folded across his chest. He was frowning when his mother came into the kitchen, the frown deepening when it became apparent that she wasn't able to see him.

We all watched as the old woman fussed about, trying to gather up the spoons, which, with her poor eyesight, she couldn't really see. When she was done, there were still errant spoons under the table and in front of the fridge, but she put the mug back on the table, gave the kitchen a last puzzled look, then switched off the overhead light and went back to her bedroom.

Zia and I stepped out of the between, back into the kitchen. Our sudden appearance startled Donald, which was kind of funny, seeing how he was the ghost and ghosts usually did the startling. But I didn't say anything because I didn't want to set us all off again—or at least it would be enough to set Zia and me off. I could feel that chemical imbalance spilling through me because she was so near—a sudden giddy need to turn sense into nonsense for the sheer fun of it—but I reminded myself why I was here. How, if I didn't fulfill my promise, I'd be beholden to a ghost for the rest of my days, and if there's one thing that cousins can't abide, it's the unpaid debt, the unfulfilled promise. That's like flying with a long chain dangling from your foot.

"How did you do that?" Donald asked.

Zia gave him a puzzled look. "Do what?"

"Disappear, then just reappear out of nowhere."

"We didn't disappear," she told him. "We were just in the between."

I thought he was going to ask her to explain that, but he changed the subject to what was obviously more often on his mind than it wasn't.

"Did you see?" he asked us. "She was standing right in front of me and she didn't even notice me. Dead or alive, she's never paid any attention to me."

"Well, you *are* a ghost," Zia said.

I nodded. "And humans can't usually see ghosts."

"A mother should be able to see her own son," he said, "whether he's a ghost or not."

"The world is full of shoulds," Zia said, "but that doesn't make them happen."

It took him a moment to work through that. When he did, he gave a slow nod.

"Here's another should," he said. "I should never have gotten my hopes up that anyone would help me."

"We didn't say we wouldn't or that we couldn't," Zia said.

I nodded. "I made you a promise."

"And cousins don't break promises," Zia added. "It's all we have for coin and what would it be worth if our word had no value?"

"So you're cousins," he said.

He didn't mean it the way we did. He was thinking of familial ties, while for us it was just an easy way to differentiate humans from people like us, whose genetic roots went back to the first days in the long ago—people who weren't bound to the one shape the way regular humans and animals are.

Instead of explaining, I just nodded.

"Show me your sister's room," Zia said.

Donald led us down the hall to Madeline's bedroom. He

122

walked through the closed door, but I stopped to open it before Zia and I followed him inside.

"It's very girly," Zia said as she took in the all the lace and dolls and the bright frothy colours. Then she pointed to the pennants and trophies. "But sporty, too."

"Not to mention clean," Donald said. "You should see my room. Mother closed the door the day I died and it hasn't been opened since."

"*I've* been in there," I said.

"But Maddy's room," he went on as though I hadn't spoken. "Mother makes sure the cleaning lady sees to it every week—before she tackles any other room in the apartment."

"Why do you think that is?" Zia asked.

"Because so far as my mother was concerned, the sun and moon rose and set on my sister Maddy."

"But *why* did she think that?"

"I don't know."

"You told me something the last time I was here," I said. "Something about how maybe you reminded her too much of your father...."

"Who abandoned us," he finished. "That's just something Maddy thought."

Zia nodded. "Well, let's find out. Did your sister call you Donald?"

"What?"

"Your sister. What did she call you?"

"Donnie."

"Okay, good. That's all I needed."

"Hey, wait!" Donald said as she pulled back the covers

and got into the bed.

Zia pretended he hadn't spoken.

"You two should hide," she said.

"But—"

"We don't want your mother to see anybody but me."

"Like she could see me."

That was true. But the mother *could* see me.

I didn't know what Zia was up to, but I went over to the closet and opened the door, pulling it almost closed it again so that I was standing in the dark in a press of dresses and skirts and tops with just a crack to peer through. Donald let out a long theatrical sigh, but after a moment he joined me.

"Mama, Mama!" Zia cried from the bed, her voice the high and frightened sound of a young girl waking from a bad dream.

Faster than she'd come into the kitchen earlier, the mother appeared in the doorway and crossed the room to the bed. She hesitated beside it, staring down at where Zia was sitting up with her arms held out for comfort. I could see the confusion in the old woman's half-blind gaze, but all it took was for Zia to call "Mama" one more time, and a mother's instinct took over. She sat on the edge of the bed, taking Zia in her arms.

"I…I was so scared, Mama," Zia said. "I dreamed I was dead."

The old woman stiffened. I saw a shiver run from her shoulders all the way down her arms and back. Then she pressed her face into Zia's hair.

"Oh, Maddy, Maddy," she said, her voice a bare whisper.

"I wish it *was* a dream."

Zia pulled back from her, but took hold of her hands.

"I *am* dead, Mama," she said. "Aren't I?"

The old woman nodded.

"But then why am I here?" Zia asked. "What keeps me here?"

"M-maybe I…I just can't let you go…."

"But you don't keep Donnie here. Why did you let him go and not me?'

"Oh, Maddy, sweetheart. Don't talk about him."

"I don't understand. Why not? He's my brother. I loved him. Didn't you love him?"

The old woman looked down at her lap.

"Mama?" Zia asked. The old woman finally lifted her head. "I…I think I loved him too much," she said.

The ghost boy had no physical presence, standing beside me here in the closet, but I could feel his sudden tension as though he were flesh and blood—a prickling flood of interest and shock and pure confusion.

"I still don't understand," Zia said.

The old woman was quiet for so long I didn't think she was going to explain. But she finally looked away from Zia, across the room, her gaze seeing into the past rather than what lay in front of her.

"Donnie was a good boy," she said. "Too good for this world, I guess, because he was taken from it while he was still so young. I knew he'd grow up to make me proud—at least I thought I did. My eyesight's bad now, sweetheart, but I think I was blinder back then because I never saw that he wouldn't get the chance to grow up at all."

Her gaze returned to Zia before Zia could speak.

"But you," the old woman said. "Oh, I could see trouble in you. You were too much like your father. Left to your own devices, I could see you turning into a little hellion. That you could be as bad as he was, if you were given half a chance. So I kept you busy—too busy to get into trouble, I thought—but I didn't do any better of a job raising you than I did him.

"You were both taken so young and I can't help but feel that the blame for that lay with me."

She fell silent, but I knew Zia wasn't going to let it go, even though we had what we needed.

The ghost boy's mother *did* remember him.

She *had* loved him.

I'd fulfilled my part of the bargain and I wanted to tell Zia to stop. I almost pushed open the closet door. I'd already raised my hand and laid my palm against the wood paneling, but Donald stopped me before I could actually give it a push.

"I need to hear this," he said. "I...I just really do."

I let my hand fall back to my side.

"But why don't you ever talk about Donnie?" Zia asked. "Why is his room closed up and forgotten and mine's like I just stepped out for a soda?"

"When I let him die," the old woman said, after another long moment of silence, "all by himself, swelled up and choking from that bee sting..." She shook her head. "I was so ashamed. There's not a day goes by that I don't think about it...about him...but I keep it locked away inside. It's my terrible secret. Better to let the world not know that I ever had a son, than that I let him die the way he did."

"Except you didn't kill him."

"No. But I did neglect him. If I'd been here instead of driving you to some piano class or gym meet or whatever it was that day, he'd still be alive."

"So it's my fault…."

"Oh no, honey. Don't even think such a thing. I was the one who made all the wrong choices. I was the one who thought he didn't need attention, but that you did. Except I was wrong about that, too. Look what happened to Donnie. And look how you turned out before…before…"

"I died."

She nodded. "You were a good girl. You were the best daughter a mother could have had. I was so proud of you, of all you'd achieved."

"And my room…"

"I keep it and your memory alive because it's the only thing left in this world that can give me any pride. It's the light that burns into the darkness and lets me forget my shame. Not always. Not for long. But even the few moments I can steal free of my shame are a blessed respite."

She fell silent again, head bowed, unable to look at what she thought was the ghost of her daughter.

Zia turned and glanced at where I was peering at her from the crack I'd made with the closet door. I knew her well enough to know what she was thinking. It was never hard. All I had to do was imagine I was in her shoes, and consider what I would say or do or think.

I turned to Donald.

"Is there anything you want to tell your mother?" I whispered.

He gave me a slow nod.

"Then just tell Zia and she'll pass it on to your mother."

He gave me another nod, but he still didn't speak.

"Donald?" I said.

"I don't know what to say. I mean, there's a million things I could say, but none of them seem to matter anymore. She's beating herself up way more than any hurt I could have wished upon her."

I reached out a comforting hand, but of course I couldn't touch him. Still, he understood the gesture. I think he even appreciated it.

"And I don't even wish it on her anymore," he added. "But then…while I feel bad about what she's going through, at the same time I still feel hurt for the way she ignored me."

I opened the door a little more, enough to catch Zia's eye. She inclined her head to show that she understood.

"I've talked to Donnie," Zia said. "In the, you know. The hereafter. Before he went on."

The old woman lifted her head and looked Zia in the eye.

"You…you have?"

Zia nodded. "He understands, but he really wishes you'd celebrate his life the way you do mine. It…hurts him to think that you never think of him."

"Oh, God, there's not a day goes by that I don't think of him."

"He knows that now."

Zia's gaze went back to me and I made a continuing

motion with my hand.

"And he wants," she went on, then caught herself. "He wanted you to know that he'll always love you. That he never held you to blame for what happened to him."

The old woman put her arms around Zia.

"Oh, my boy," she said. "My poor, poor boy."

"He wants you to be happy," Zia said. "We both do."

The woman shook her head against Zia's shoulder.

"I don't even know the meaning of the word anymore," she said.

"Will you at least try?"

The old woman sat up and dabbed at her eyes with the sleeve of her housecoat.

"How does one even begin?" she said.

"Well, sometimes, if you pretend you're happy, you can trick yourself into at least feeling better."

"I don't think I could do that."

"Try by celebrating our lives," Zia said. "Remember both your children with love and joy. There'll always be sadness, but try to remember that it wasn't always that way."

"No," the old woman said slowly. "You're right. It wasn't. I don't know if you can even remember, but we were once a happy family. But then Ted left and I had to go back to work, and you children...you were robbed of the life you should have had."

"It happens," Zia said—a touch too matter-of-factly for the ghost of a dead girl, I thought, but the old woman didn't appear to notice.

"It's time for me to go, Mama," Zia added. "Will you let

me go?"

"Can't you stay just a little longer?"

"No," Zia said. "Let me walk you back to your bed."

She got up and the two of them left the room, the old woman leaning on Zia.

"I'm going to wake up in the morning," I heard the old woman say from the hall, "and this will all have just been a dream."

"Not if you don't want it to," Zia told her. "You've got a strong will. Look how long you kept me from moving on. You can remember this—everything we've talked about—for what it really was. And if you try hard, you can be happy again."

* * *

Donald and I waited in the bedroom until Zia returned.

"Is she asleep?" I asked.

Zia nodded. "I think all of this exhausted her." She turned to Donald. "So, how do you feel now?"

"I feel strange," he said. "Like there's something tugging at me...trying to pull me away."

"That's because it's time for you to move on," I told him.

"I guess."

"You're remembered now," Zia said. "That's what was holding you back before."

He gave a slow nod. "Listening to her...it didn't make me feel a whole lot better. I mean, I understand now, but..."

"Life's not very tidy," Zia said, "so I suppose there's no reason for death to be any different."

"I..."

He was harder to hear. I gave him a careful study and

130

realized he'd grown much more insubstantial.

"It's hard to hold on," he said. "To stay here."

"Then don't," Zia told him.

I nodded. "Just let go."

"But I'm...scared."

Zia and I looked at each other.

"We were here at the beginning of things," she said, turning back to him, "before Raven pulled the world out of that old pot of his. We've been in the great beyond that lies on the other side of the long ago. It's..."

She looked at me.

"It's very peaceful there," I finished for her.

"I don't want to go to Hell," he said. "What if I go to Hell?"

His voice was very faint now and I could hardly make him out in the gloom of the room.

"You won't go to Hell," I said.

I didn't know if there was a Heaven or a Hell, or *what* lay on the other side of living. Maybe nothing. Maybe everything. But there was no reason to tell him that. He wanted certainty.

"Hell's for bad people," I told him, "and you're just a poor kid who got stung by a bee."

I saw the fading remnants of his mouth moving, but I couldn't make out the words. And then he was gone.

I looked at Zia.

"I don't feel any better," I said. "Did we help him?"

"I don't know. We must have. We did what he wanted."

"I suppose."

"And he's gone on now."

She linked her arm in mine and walked me into the between.

"I had this idea for a store," she said.

"I know. Where you don't sell anything. Instead people just bring you stuff."

She nodded. "It was a pretty dumb idea."

"It wasn't that bad. I've had worse."

"I know you have."

We stepped out of the between onto the fire escape outside the apartment. I looked across the city. Dawn was still a long way off, but everywhere I could see the lights of the city, the headlights of cars moving between the tall canyons of the buildings.

"I think we need to go somewhere and make a big happy noise," Zia said. "We have to go mad and dance and sing and do cartwheels along the telephone wires like we're famous trapeze artists."

"Because…?"

"Because it's better than feeling sad."

So we did.

And later we returned to the Rookery and woke up all the cousins until every black bird in every tree was part of our loud croaking and raspy chorus. I saw Lucius open the window of his library and look out. When he saw Zia and me leading the cacophony from our high perch in one of the old oak trees in the backyard, he just shook his head and closed the window again.

But not before I saw him smile to himself.

* * *

132

I went back to the old woman's apartment a few weeks later to see if the ghost boy was really gone. I meant to go sooner, but something distracting always seemed to come up before I could actually get going.

Zia might tell me about a hoard of Mardi Gras beads she'd found in a dumpster, and then off we'd have to go to collect them all, bringing them back to the Rookery where we festooned the trees with them until Lucius finally asked us to take them down, his voice polite, but firm, the way it always got when he felt we'd gone the step too far.

Or Chlöe might call us into the house because she'd made us each a sugar pie, big fat pies with much more filling than crust because we liked the filling the best. We didn't even need the crust, except then it would just be pudding, which we also liked, but it wasn't pie, now, was it?

Once we had to go into the faraway to help our friend Jilly, because we promised we would if she ever called us. So when she did, we went to her. That promise had never been like a chain dangling from our feet when we flew, but it still felt good to be done with it.

But finally I remembered the ghost boy and managed to not get distracted before I could make my way to his mother's apartment. When I got there, they were both gone, the old woman and her dead son. Instead, there was a young man I didn't recognize sitting in the kitchen when I stepped out of the between. He was in the middle of spooning ice cream into a bowl.

"Do you want some?" he asked.

He was one of those people who didn't seem the least bit

133

surprised to find me appearing out of thin air in the middle of his kitchen. Tomorrow morning, he probably wouldn't even remember I'd been here.

"What flavour is it?" I asked.

"Chocolate swirl with bits of Oreo cookies mixed in."

"I'd love some," I told him and got myself a bowl from the cupboard.

He filled my bowl with a generous helping and we both spent a few moments enjoying the ice cream. I looked down the hall as I ate and saw all the cardboard boxes. My gaze went back to the young man's face.

"What's your name?" I asked him.

"Nels."

He didn't ask me my name, but I didn't mind.

"This is a good invention," I said holding up a spoonful of ice cream. "Chocolate and ice cream and cookies all mixed up in the same package."

"It's not new. They've had it for ages."

"But it's still good."

"Mmm."

"So what happened to the old woman who lived here?" I asked.

"I didn't know her," he told me. "The realtor brought me by a couple of days ago and I liked the place, so I rented it. I'm pretty sure he said she'd passed away."

So much for her being happy. But maybe there was something else on the other side of living. Maybe she and her ghost boy and her daughter were all together again and she *was* happy.

It was a better ending to the story than others I could imagine.

"So," I asked Nels, "are you happy?"

He paused with a spoonful of ice cream halfway to his mouth. "What?"

"Do you have any ghosts?"

"Everybody's got ghosts."

"Really?"

He nodded. "I suppose one of the measures of how you live your life is how well you make your peace with them."

My bowl was empty, but I didn't fill it up again. I stood up from the table.

"Do you want some help unpacking?" I asked.

"Nah. I'm good. Are you off?"

"You know me," I said, although of course he didn't. "Places to go, people to meet. Things to do."

He smiled. "Well, don't be a stranger. Or at least not any stranger than you already are."

I laughed.

"You're a funny man, Nels," I said.

And then I stepped away into the between. I stood there for a few moments, watching him.

He got up from the table, returned the ice cream to the freezer and washed out the bowls and utensils we'd used. When he was done, he walked into the hall and picked up a box, which he took into the living room, out of my sight.

I could tell that he'd already forgotten me.

"Goodbye, Nels," I said, though he couldn't hear me. "Goodbye, Ghost Boy. Goodbye, old lady." I knew they couldn't hear me, either.

Then I stepped from the between, out onto the fire escape. I unfolded black wings and flew back to the Rookery, singing loudly all the way.

At least I thought of it as singing.

As I got near Stanton Street, a man waiting for his dog to relieve itself looked up to see me go by.

"Goddamned crows," he said.

He took a plastic bag out of his pocket and deftly bagged his dog's poop.

I sang louder, a laughing arpeggio of croaking notes.

Being happy was better than not, I decided. And it was certainly better than scooping up dog poop. If I was ever to write a story, the way that Christy did, it would be very short. And I'd only have the one story because after it, I wouldn't need any more.

It would go like this:

Once upon a time, they all lived happily ever after. The end.

That's a much better sort of story than the messy ones that make up our lives. At least that's what I think.

But I wouldn't want to live in that story because that would be too boring. I'd rather be caught up in the clutter of living, flying high above the streets and houses, making a joyful noise.

AFTERWORD

There's a truism when it comes to the creative arts: If you put the work in every day, from time to time the universe will give you a gift. It doesn't happen often, but when it does it really does feel special. It's when the song comes to you—melody and words all at once. When a story flows through you and you hardly need to change a word. Sometimes it's a character who just steps into your head and everything about them has the weight of reality—you just *know* them.

But it only happens if you put the work in.

The original crow girls story was like that. It dates back to a time when, every Christmas, I would write a story as a gift for my wife MaryAnn, but which we then sent out as a Christmas card in the form of a chapbook. While most stories I wrote were commissioned for various anthologies, the chapbooks had no preset length or theme. I just told whatever story I felt like writing.

So back in 1995 I opened a file and typed, "People have a

funny way of remembering where they've been, who they were. Facts fall by the wayside." And the rest of the story just flowed out of me without my having to do much more than get the words on the screen.

"Crow Girls" was a double gift. Not only did the story come as a gift, but so did Maida and Zia. I knew them well before I ever wrote a word because they stepped fully realized out of the shadows of my mind, and I fell in love with them. They're sweet and silly, loyal to a fault, but with an underlying steel to their demeanor if you cross them or do something they consider to be morally wrong.

As I mentioned in the new afterword for my novel *Someplace to Be Flying*, what I couldn't foresee was how much my readers would take to them. Over the years, many fans have shown up at events dressed as crow girls. Sometimes they don't even have to dress up or change anything about themselves at all, and that's all the more fun.

As the original wild spirits, the crow girls probably don't make good role models (for instance, just consider how they like to help themselves to things that belong to others), but I'm delighted that so many of my readers, especially young women, have taken them to heart.

Because the crow girls care for each other. They don't take crap from anybody. They live in the moment and pay attention to *everything*.

Now, that strikes me as behaviour that we should all embrace.

* * *

For some time now readers have been asking for story

collections centered around their favourite Newford characters. The crow girls are almost invariably at the top of their lists, so we decided to start these Newford Stories collections with them.

A number of the other regular members of the Newford repertory company show up here, but at the forefront of each story are these two little wild girls with their big personalities.

I like to think that, male or female, old or young, no matter what one's cultural background, sexual orientation, or religious leaning, we all have a little bit of crow girl inside us.

* * *

A very special thanks to Tara Larsen Chang for providing us with her charming take on crow girls, and to Joanne Harris for taking the time from her busy schedule to provide an introduction. If you've never read her, you're in for a treat. I recommend you start with *Chocolat* or *Blackberry Wine*, though you can't go wrong with any of her books.

You can read more about the crow girls and other corbae in my novel *Someplace to Be Flying*.

ABOUT THE AUTHOR

Charles de Lint is a full-time writer and musician who makes his home in Ottawa, Canada. This author of more than seventy adult, young adult, and children's books has won the World Fantasy, Aurora, Sunburst, and White Pine awards, among others. Modern Library's Top 100 Books of the 20th Century poll, voted on by readers, put eight of de Lint's books among the top 100. De Lint is also a poet, artist, songwriter, performer and folklorist, and he writes a monthly book-review column for The Magazine of Fantasy & Science Fiction. For more information, visit his web site at www.charlesdelint.com

You can also connect with him at:
www.facebook.com/pages/Charles-de-Lint/218001537221
twitter.com/cdelint
cdelint.tumblr.com/

Made in the USA
Monee, IL
21 June 2021